Family Business

The Children

Book IV

Family Business Series

Family Business IV

The Children

Vanessa
Miller

Book IV
Family Business Series

Vanessa Miller

www.vanessamiller.com

Printed in the United States of America
© 2017 by Vanessa Miller

Praise Unlimited Enterprises
Charlotte, NC

Other Books by Vanessa Miller

Family Business Book I
Family Business II - Sword of Division
Family Business III - Love And Honor
Family Business IV - The Children
Sunshine And Rain
Rain in the Promised Land
After the Rain
How Sweet The Sound
Heirs of Rebellion
Heaven Sent
Feels Like Heaven
Heaven on Earth
The Best of All
Better for Us
Her Good Thing
Long Time Coming
A Promise of Forever Love
A Love for Tomorrow
Yesterday's Promise
Forgotten
Forgiven
Forsaken
Rain for Christmas (Novella)
Through the Storm
Rain Storm
Latter Rain

Abundant Rain

Former Rain

Anthologies (Editor)

Keeping the Faith

Have A Little Faith

This Far by Faith

EBOOKS

Love Isn't Enough

A Mighty Love

The Blessed One (Blessed and Highly Favored series)

The Wild One (Blessed and Highly Favored Series)

The Preacher's Choice (Blessed and Highly Favored Series)

The Politician's Wife (Blessed and Highly Favored Series)

The Playboy's Redemption (Blessed and Highly Favored Series)

Tears Fall at Night (Praise Him Anyhow Series)

Joy Comes in the Morning (Praise Him Anyhow Series)

A Forever Kind of Love (Praise Him Anyhow Series)

Ramsey's Praise (Praise Him Anyhow Series)

Escape to Love (Praise Him Anyhow Series)

Praise For Christmas (Praise Him Anyhow Series)

His Love Walk (Praise Him Anyhow Series)

Could This Be Love (Praise Him Anyhow Series)

Song of Praise (Praise Him Anyhow Series)

Prologue

There was a day when the sons of God came to present themselves before the Lord, and Satan was also among them. And the Lord said to Satan, "From where do you come?"

Satan answered the Lord and said, "From going to and fro on the earth, and from walking back and forth on it."

The Lord said to Satan, "Have you considered My servant Angel, how there is none like her on the earth, and how she and her son Obadiah Damerae Shepherd fear God and shun evil?"

Satan answered the Lord, "Do they fear God for nothing? Angel's husband is a criminal, trafficking drugs and ordering murders and yet You have made a hedge around the entire Shepherd family, and around all that they have on every side? You have not only blessed the work of her hands, but her husband's as well. His possessions have increased greatly and not once has he ever bowed a knee to the Almighty. But if You stretch out Your hand and touch all that they have, Demetrius and Angel will surely curse You to Your face."

And the Lord said to Satan, "Behold, all that they have is in your power; only do not lay a hand on Demetrius and Angel."

Satan went out from the presence of the Lord and stirred up the anger of an old foe in order to crush Angel and her bible thumping son before they could convert anymore of the Shepherd family away from doing evil on the earth.

1

The first blow came on Friday afternoon, Demetrius was sitting in his office reviewing the plans to ship millions of dollars to the Columbians for the drug shipment they had managed to get through customs. In the ten years he'd been doing business with the Columbians only one shipment had ever been detected by the DEA. The officer who detected the shipment was now able to buy his wife that four-bedroom dream house she'd been begging him for and take his family on lavish vacations.

Demetrius knew how to move money and how to pay off detectives. He also knew how to process dope and get it on the street. His father, Don Shepherd had taught him well. But even as Don was finishing a ten-year prison stint in federal prison, Demetrius was growing weary of his father's legacy. He longed to be at peace with his family and not have to look over his back all the time.

"Where you at? Where your mind at today?" Moe, his right-hand man and boy for life asked him.

Demetrius leaned back in his chair. As his eyes drifted towards the window, he told Moe, "I'm just over it... this wasn't supposed to be my life. Know what I mean, Man?"

Moe shot back at him, "Your problem is, this was exactly what your life was supposed to be. Don groomed you for this life since you were in knee socks and short pants."

"Yeah, but that was when we were just in the lottery game."

"But then, Moe did air quotation marks, the real lottery came in and took over. Nobody wanted a number's man when they could make more with the government's lottery."

Rolling his eyes, and then laughing at a memory, Demetrius said, "I went on my first numbers run with my old man when I was just four years old. Can you imagine what Angel would have said if I had introduced my sons to street life like that?"

"Man, Angel would have slapped some Holy oil on you and then knocked you in the head with a cast iron skillet, all in the name of Jesus." Moe laughed until he fell out of his seat.

"It's not funny, Moe. Numbers running was one thing, but I never want any of my sons to see me caught up in street life like this. There's a better way to earn a dollar and I'm going to make sure each one of them figure that out." Demetrius stood and walked over to the window. He stared out at the strip mall he had designed and built. This place was supposed to be his reward for running numbers all those years with his dad...he was supposed to go legit and take care of his wife and kids. He was supposed to keep his family out of harm's way.

Demetrius turned back to Moe and acknowledged, "It took a long time for me to forgive my father for getting me caught up with the Columbians."

"Well, he'll be home in about what, two-three months? You can hand this business over to him and just walk away."

"Yeah, but what am I going to do when I just walk away? This strip mall was my ticket out. But now every business in the mall, accept for the restaurant KeKe manages is knee deep in the money laundering business. So, this place I built from the ground up is not mine anymore, it too belongs to Don Shepherd."

Moe jumped up, pointing out the window. "Fire!"

"What?" Demetrius turned to where Moe had directed and indeed, one of the buildings in his strip mall was on fire.

"This place ain't gon' be nobodies if we don't get the fire department out here to contain the blaze." Moe used the office phone to dial 911. When he hung up, he told Demetrius, "They're in route. We better get over there."

When Demetrius and Moe stepped outside they could clearly see that it was the African American Art store that was burning. All at once, Moe shouted, "The money!"

Demetrius shouted, "Dee!"

Two different realities were happening at the same time and they both could affect life as Demetrius knew it. First, he had brought his son Demetrius Jr. (Dee) to work with him today because the boy had graduated high school four months ago and still wasn't doing anything with his life. The guy who ran the African American Art store was on vacation this week so Demetrius had Dee running the store.

The second issue with that building was the storage room directly behind it was where Demetrius kept bundles of money that needed to be sent to the Columbians. If that money burnt up, the Columbians weren't just going to take a write off. He told Moe, "Get the truck, you get the money and I'm going to get my son."

"Demetrius, you can't go in the front of that building. Look how fast it's burning. Just wait on the fireman."

Demetrius was already running towards the building, "Just go get the money," he yelled back to Moe. Demetrius was not about to stand by and wait on some fireman to roll up here and pull his son's lifeless body out of the store. When he reached the store and put his hand on the door, it was hot to the touch. But he didn't concern himself with that as he flung open the door. "Dee! Dee! Are you in here?"

There was no response from Dee but he heard Moe holler from the storage unit in the back of the store, "The door is wide open. Somebody has been in here."

Demetrius couldn't concern himself with that right now. The fire was destroying all of the beautiful artwork. Smoke was covering the room and yet, Demetrius persisted. He got down on the floor and crawled around trying to find his son. "Dee, can you hear me?"

Still nothing from Dee. But a piece of the roof fell down from the back and Demetrius heard Moe yell. "Get out of there, Demetrius. The roof is about to collapse."

Demetrius ignored the danger signs; all he was thinking about was getting to his son. If Dee was unconscious in this fire, and he backed out and just left him in here, he might as well put a bullet in his skull because he wouldn't be able to live with that.

Closing his mouth, trying his best not to inhale too much smoke, Demetrius crawled around the flames that were in front of him and made his way behind the counter. He thought that Dee might be stretched out behind the counter, but his son wasn't there. It was a small store so Demetrius comforted himself with the knowledge that his son must have escaped. He just didn't understand why Dee didn't run over to his office to tell him about the fire. He turned to crawl back to the door but a piece of the roof fell just a foot or so away from him.

"What just happened?" Moe hollered from the other side of the enclosed room.

Just then Demetrius heard the fire truck headed their way. "Another piece of the roof fell."

"I'm coming around front. I need to get you out of there."

"No! Get the money. I'll get myself out of here."

"Demetrius man, I'm not just gon' let you die over there."

"If I can't pay the Columbians I'm a dead man anyway. Just do your job. Let the firemen help me out of here." The people he did business with wouldn't just kill him if they thought he was stealing from them, they'd torture his family first, while he watched and then they'd kill him. And Demetrius would rather die in this fire than let that happen.

The flames were too high to crawl through, so Demetrius stood up and tried to jump off to the side of the flames. He almost made it, but the leg of his pants got caught on a pallet and he fell to the ground just as another piece of the roof came tumbling down. Demetrius rolled to get away from the tumbling debris, but he rolled directly into a blaze of fire.

While Demetrius was trying to pat the fire out, he noticed that his foot was stuck on something and he couldn't get up. The fire was raging like an angry lover who was about to extract revenge. The entire ceiling was about to collapse on him. All Demetrius could think was, "I'm not ready to
    die."

Then he saw a figure like a man standing in the fire. "Dee! Oh God, please no!" The figure disappeared and suddenly, Demetrius could move his leg.

"Help... man on fire... help!" Demetrius could hear Moe yelling from outside the door.

Demetrius could barely see what was in front of him anymore. But he lowered his head and started crawling toward the sounds that were coming from outside. The closer he got to the door, the more he coughed. His lungs felt like they were on fire. His body felt weak, like he couldn't move another inch and then he collapsed.

~~~

When Angel arrived on the scene, Demetrius was seated on the back of an ambulance getting his arm bandaged and wrapped. "What in the world happened to you?"

"I thought I was about to die, that's what happened to me," Demetrius told his wife as she rushed to his side.

"I saw it on the news. Looked like the fire was going to destroy the entire right side of the strip mall." Angel took a minute to study her husband. He said he almost died, but thank God there weren't any burns on any part of his body accept the arm the paramedic was wrapping.

"I'm alright bae. A fireman pulled me out before the fire did too much damage."

"Why didn't y'all just call the fire department in the first place?"

"We did," Moc told her.

"Then why didn't y'all let them do their job? Were you trying to get people out of the store or something?" When he didn't respond, her voice got louder, "Did you hear my question?"

"We'll talk about it later." Demetrius stood and rolled what was left of his sleeve down.

"It means, that I'm tired and I don't want to talk right now. I just want to go home."

Angel folded her arms across her chest. "No, I don't want to be put off like you always do. I heard on the news that some type of pipe bomb was thrown inside the store. Why would someone do that? What's going on here?"

"Calm down, Angel. Everything is fine." Demetrius put Angel's hand in his and walked her back to her white Mercedes.

"What about us, Demetrius? Do you think they'll try to set our house on fire again?" Ten years ago, their house had gone up in flames and Demetrius sent her to stay with her parents while he built another home for their family, complete with a security check point. Now, anyone trying to get anywhere near their home had to be approved and the security guard had to open the gate for entry. That entry point and the cameras Demetrius had installed around the house helped her to feel safe in her home. But this firebombing had unnerved Angel and Demetrius wasn't being fair to her by constantly keeping secrets.

"I don't know who did this, baby. But I promise you that our home is safe. Nothing is going to happen to you or the kids." Demetrius opened her car door, but Angel wasn't ready to leave.

"How can you promise something like that, Demetrius?" She pointed at his bandaged arm. "You couldn't even protect yourself."

"You're being hysterical, Angel. This is not like you. So, please take a deep breath and let me handle my business."

"You told me that you almost died. How am I supposed to hear something like that and just go home, with no questions asked?" Her lip was quivering as she put a hand on his head. "I need to know that we're going to be okay."

"I've kept our family safe this long, Angel. What makes you think anything has changed?"

He wasn't going to tell her anything more than he already had. This was their normal dance. As long as Demetrius was leading her in the dance it would always end with unanswered questions. "I'm going to pick up the kids. How much longer will you be?"

"The detectives have a few questions they want to ask and then Moe and I need to take care of some business."

"Sounds like you're going to be a while. Are you going to grab dinner or do you want me to make you something?" Angel was trying to carry on as normal a conversation as possible even though her husband was standing in front of her with a fire bruised arm, which occurred because one of his stores had been fire bombed. But this is the life she had signed up for all those years ago when she agreed to marry the son of a gangster.

When they first married, Angel had only thought of her love for Demetrius and nothing of the love she had once had in her heart for God. But ten years ago, all that changed. The Lord came into her life and completely changed her. Now she spent every night of her life praying that Demetrius would come to know the God she served and that God would get so deep on the inside of Demetrius that he would no longer desire to please his earthly father. She yearned for the day her husband would finally acknowledge and trust his heavenly Father.

2

On Sunday morning, Angel got out of bed and went into her walk-in closet to pick out an outfit to wear to church as she had done every Sunday morning for the past ten years. After finding her dress or pantsuit, Angel would then get down on her knees and pray to God, asking Him to soften Demetrius' heart towards the things of God. Angel wanted her entire family saved by the blood of the Lamb. She wanted every member of the Shepherd household in church on Sunday mornings.

But this Sunday was different, as Angel was looking at one of the dresses, trying to decide if she was in the mood for red today, Demetrius hollered, "Pick me out a suit to wear."

Angel's hands went straight to her hips. "Where are you going this early in the morning?" She didn't bother disguising the irritation that she felt. Angel hated when Demetrius hung out with his friends on Sunday morning rather than going to church with his family.

"I was going to church with you," he shot back. "But if you'd rather I keep laying here. I guess I can do that instead."

Angel popped out of the closet. "Are you serious?"

He nodded.

"You really want to go to church with me this morning?" Angel had been praying for this very thing for ten years, but she still couldn't believe what she was hearing.

Demetrius raised up on an elbow. He grinned at his wife as he said, "Look at yo' fine self. I should have been down at that church house with you."

"Is this about the fire?" As soon as the words were out of her mouth, Angel wanted to take them back. Why was she questioning his motives...what was that old saying, 'don't look a gift horse in the mouth'.

"I will admit that I'm feeling like I should show up in God's house this morning to let Him know I'm thankful that I'm among the living and breathing."

"I'll get your suit." This time she rushed back into the closet without saying another word. This day was a long time coming, so she wasn't going to get in God's way. She lifted her hands and gave praise, "Thank You, Lord," she whispered and then walked back out of the closet carrying a navy-blue suit with a gray shirt for her man.

"Is this okay?"

"Yeah, if that's what you want me to wear. Then I'm good."

"I have a blue and gray dress that I'll wear so we can look like the Shepherd twins." Angel smiled at him, but she said nothing else about it. She didn't want to make him uncomfortable with his decision to attend church and then back out. Angel had prayed a long time for Demetrius' salvation, she was getting excited at the thought that this might be the day the Lord had planned from the foundation of the world for Demetrius to fellowship with his heavenly Father.

When she stepped out of her bedroom and closed the door, Angel danced her way to her children's room, passing out church clothes and helping Dodi bathe and get dressed.

"Why you dancing like that, Mama?" Dodi asked as she handed her a pair of pink stockings to put on.

"Oh, I was just thinking of the goodness of the Lord and how He answers prayers."

Dodi looked at her strange, but Angel didn't care. She was happy. Today was going to be good for the Shepherd family. With all the stress Dee had been causing them since he turned eighteen, Angel was grateful that the Lord would allow her to see the day her husband stepped a foot in the house of God. She went downstairs to make breakfast with a smile on her face.

As the smell of the bacon and eggs drifted throughout the house her children made their way to the kitchen. DeMarcus had graduated from college and was now playing professionally in the NFL so he was not at the table with the rest of the children anymore. Dee had lost his mind on his eighteenth birthday so he basically only lived at home on a part-time basis, having chosen to hang out with his girlfriend and his boys, rather than his family. Even though Angel said many prayers for Dee, she did not set a plate at the table for her son.

She filled their plates with eggs and bacon and tried to be thankful that she still had three of her children at home. Dontae was fifteen and not only did he look as if his father had spit him out, he was also in love with the game of baseball. Demetrius loved it. He took Dontae to every practice because he swears up and down that Dontae will be going pro just like his big brother.

Angel didn't know if Dontae was going pro or not, she was just grateful that father and son had something that they could share. Dontae needed that space in time with his father because Dee was taking up most of Angel and Demetrius' time these days with all of his antics. Demetrius' name sake was only eighteen but had already been arrested twice, thankful both instances were for petty crimes. But Angel had a feeling that Dee was about to get in more trouble than his father would be able to get him out of, so she kept praying and talking to that boy until she was hoarse from talking so much.

Demetrius didn't do much talking where Dee was concerned. Lately, he'd been laying hands on their son and Angel didn't like it at all. Don Shepherd had been a hard man and he'd raised Demetrius with an iron fist. Now Demetrius was doing the same to Dee. Angel had tried reasoning with her husband, but they were not seeing eye to eye on how to deal with Dee.

Demetrius strutted into the kitchen with his three-piece pin stripped lavender suit with hat to match that made him look more like pimp-daddy than a man on his way to church. But Angel didn't demand that he go back upstairs and change in to the navy-blue suit she had laid out for him. She walked over to her husband and planted a soft, wet kiss on his lips and then told him how thankful she was to be able to walk into church with her man today.

"Wait," Dontae looked puzzled. "Daddy's going to church with us?"

Demetrius buttoned his jacket and glanced over at his son. "Don't you think it's about time your old man checked out this church y'all love so much?"

"Yeah Daddy, way past time," Ten-year-old Dam told him.

"Way, way past time," Dodi said.

Angel smiled at her youngest child. The girl Demetrius wanted so badly that he'd been willing to open his heart to a child he had never wanted. Angel had given birth to five children, but there had been a time in their marriage that Demetrius thought he was only the biological father to three of them. Her first son DeMarcus was eighteen months when she met Demetrius so no surprise there. But even though Demetrius was not DeMarcus' biological father, he loved DeMarcus just as if he came from his own seed.

19

Their fourth son, Dam had been the issue that almost destroyed their marriage. Yes, Angel had been raped by DeMarcus' father. It had broken Demetrius' spirit because he wasn't around to save her from that attack. Demetrius' failure to save Angel was the very thing that lead her to God. She finally realized the Demetrius was never meant to be her savior, but there was One who would always come to her rescue…Jesus.

Demetrius had demanded that she abort their baby because he couldn't be sure the child was his and he was not willing to raise another one of Frankie's children, no matter how much he truly loved DeMarcus. Angel had wanted to please Demetrius and to get their marriage back to a happy place, so she drove to the abortion clinic, and to this day she was still thankful that she took that trip, because that was where she met a woman named Patricia Harding. Patricia told her that God had a plan for her son and that Obadiah Damerae Shepherd, whom they affectionately call Dam, would do mighty exploits for the Lord.

Angel had grown up as a preacher's kid. The life that she'd been living with Demetrius, who had grown up as a gangster's kid was so very different than what she had known in her parent's home. But she still knew and understood the voice of the Lord when she heard it. Angel repented for even the thought of killing her baby and she fell on her knees and declared Jesus as the Lord of her life from that day forward.

Things with her and Demetrius didn't improve simply because Angel had become a servant of the Lord. As a matter of fact, their problems only became magnified. Angel and Demetrius didn't live in the same house on a consistent basis for three years after she gave her life to the Lord. Angel stayed at her parent's home. She gave birth to Dam and continued to live with her parents until Demetrius agreed to allow their son in his home. Through it all, Angel kept praying and despite her best efforts to stop loving Demetrius, she kept on loving him. By the time Demetrius discovered the truth, that he was Dam's biological father, Angel had given birth to Dodi, their last child. The girl Demetrius so desperately wanted.

"Where is Dee?" Demetrius inquired as Angel sat his plate in front of him.

She shrugged.

"That boy hasn't been home in two nights. He knows I'm looking for him so he's hiding out."

She patted him on the shoulder. "I'm praying about it."

"That's good. You keep praying and I'm going to put my foot up his-"

"Demetrius!"

"I'm serious, Angel. That boy is up to no good and I'm putting a stop to this mess right now." Demetrius reached for his tie, getting ready to take it off.

Angel put her hand over his, her eyes implored him. "Don't do this, Demetrius. Not now. Come to church with me like we planned. We can find Dee after service."

Taking a deep breath, Demetrius removed his hand from his tie and nodded. "I'm sorry bae. I said I was going to church this morning and that's exactly what I'm going to do."

"Thanks hon. I know you're worried about Dee and I am too. But I have decided to put that boy in the Lord's hands because He is the only One that will be able to turn Dee around."

Demetrius shook his head. "I've tried to shelter these kids so they'd never know anything about my business or the street life, but seems to me that Dee is running to the street life faster than I ever did and Don Shepherd is my daddy."

For just a moment Angel wondered if she had made her biggest mistake when she named Dee after his father. Dee would spend the rest of his life trying to be just like his father? God help them all if that's the case.

~~~

"Hey Little Dee, what it do?"

Dee clasps hands with Willie Pierce, one of the biggest street dealers in the city. "You know."

"What bring you out this early on a Sunday morning," Willie asked.

"Looking for Day-Day. He's holding something for me."

"Yeah, he told me about that biz' y'all got going. I wish I could let you get product from me. But your daddy would kill me."

"Don't worry 'bout it. I know you get your product from my dad. I wouldn't put you out there like that."

"He's got the best cut in town. What Day-Day's selling ain't half as good as what I've got."

Dee hit his pocket. "My dollars are good. So, you gon' sell it to me or what?"

Willie thought about it for a moment. Looked around to see if anyone else was in earshot. "Your daddy has put the word out on you, Dee. I'm surprised Day-Day is taking a chance on selling to you. But they don't sell to him, so he has to get his stuff at higher prices. You need to check Day-Day's motives before doing business with him…you got me?"

"Yeah, I got you, but it still sounds like you're not getting ready to do business with me and I know for sure that my daddy ain't about to do business with me. So, I've got to take my dollars where they're wanted."

Shaking his head, Willie told him, "I tried to warn your little rock head. You don't want to listen. Go on then. Day-Day is around the corner."

Dee walked off, he had business to take care of. He didn't need some old-head trying to school him instead of getting him what he needed. Day-Day was on the street corner, leaned up against a poll as Dee stepped to him.

"What's up, Little Dee?"

All of these cats called him 'Little Dee" but Dee was planning to shock the world and show them all that there was nothing little about him. He was just his daddy's son, he could make moves and make things happen for himself. They would see, then cats like Willie would be coming to him and begging for a seat at the table. "You got my stuff or what?"

"Oh, no small talk for you, huh? Day-Day took the tooth pick out of his mouth and grinned at him.

"I've got a lot to do today, so I just want to get what I came for and get out of here."

"You think I'm gon' stand on the corner with a kilo in my hand?"

"Naw, naw, I didn't think that. Where you got it?"

"Follow me." Day-Day took off down the street. He limped as he walked because of the bullet that was still lodged in his upper thigh.

"Whatever happened to that dude who shot you?" Dee asked, curious about the incident.

"How did they say it in that old gangster movie my granddaddy used to watch all the time...he's sleeping with the fishes."

"Huh?" Dee didn't get it.

"Put it this way Young Blood, you don't ever have to worry about him rolling up on you with a gun, believe that."

Getting the gist, Dee nodded and laughed like death was a funny ha-ha kind of thing.

They reached their destination and Day-Day said, "Step into my office," which was more like a dilapidated trap house.

From what Dee knew of these trap houses, addicts usually were all over the floor or walking the floor like zombies looking for their next fix. This might be Sunday but Dee found it odd that no one else was inside the house.

"Wait right here, Little Dee. Let me get that bag and I'll be right back."

Something in Dee's gut told him to run. Something didn't smell right, but Dee was new to the game and it wasn't like he could call his daddy and ask for pointers. Dee took a few steps toward the front door and turned the knob. Just as he was opening the door Day-Day came back into the room.

"Hey man, where you going? We got business to take care of."

"I'm out. Got to get back home." Dee swung the door wide open and rushed down the steps.

Day-Day was on his heels. "You can't leave like that. I got your product, so cough up my cheddar. I'm out here tryin' to eat."

Day-Day stepped to Dee like he was trying to intimidate him. But Dee was no punk. He was a Shepherd through and through. Dee shoved Day-Day off him and put his hand to his pocket like he was about to pull out something. "You gon' have to get fed off of some other sucka in these streets. Something stinks about this deal and I ain't interested." He cocked his head to the side. "Now, are you gon' get out of my way or am I gon' have to show you a few things my granddaddy taught me?"

At the mention of Don Shepherd, Day-Day backed up. The streets didn't fear Demetrius like they feared Don Shepherd. Word had got around that Demetrius had developed heart and that he'd even let a man live who'd kidnapped his son. But every single hustler knew that Don Shepherd would have gutted the man and then stood there and watched as the birds picked at the dead man's flesh.

"I didn't think you wanted to try me." Dee was feeling himself, like he was king of the world...thinking he'd be able to take the streets like his granddaddy had, wouldn't nobody stop him, because he was a Shepherd and that name meant something. He hadn't moved but a few inches away from Day-Day when he heard police sirens. He turned and looked as the car stopped in front of the trap house.

The police officer jumped out of the car and yelled, "Don't move! Hands up!"

All Dee could think of was that his Dad would kill him if he got arrested again. He looked at the officer, thought about putting his hands up, but then the officer slipped as he tried to step up on the curb. Dee didn't hesitate, he just kicked up dust and ran.

Willie Pierce was standing one block over watching everything go down. His loyalties belonged to the Shepherd family because they sold him product every month on the regular. Once he didn't have enough, and they helped him by collecting on the back end. He took out his cell phone and made a call. Then he walked up on Day-Day to make sure that he wasn't turning snitch on little Dee.

3

As a child, Demetrius' mother read bible verses to him. But he had never been a church goer. When his mom died, there had been no more talk of God in his house. His larger-than-life father never took Demetrius to church. Demetrius felt odd walking through the church doors, wondering if God would strike him down for daring to enter the house of God after all the dirt he'd done. But from the time he received the first hug from the greeter as he entered the sanctuary and then began listening to the praise and worship team, he felt at ease…like maybe God was okay with him being here. After all, the man upstairs let him survive that fire, didn't He?

Tears streamed down Angel's face as praise and worship went forth. Demetrius acknowledged that he was also feeling emotional. The words of the song hit him like nothing else had as the choir sang, 'Because of love, you placed yourself in harm's way. Demetrius remembered all the times he'd come so close to death and each time it seemed like some invisible force was pulling him out of harm's way.

Was it God's love that got him out of that store without being burnt beyond recognition? Angel prayed for him all the time, Demetrius knew that. But what awed him most, was the thought that no matter how dirty and wrong he'd been through the years, God had still been looking out for him.

As the song ended, he wiped at his eyes. As Demetrius sat down he kept wondering if God could really love a man like him. And if so, why?

Demetrius put an arm around Angel and pulled her closer to him. If he didn't know anything else, he knew that God most likely wouldn't have done anything for him if Angel had not spent so many nights on her knees praying for him.

"You okay?" Angel asked him.

"Yeah baby, I'm good." Demetrius watched as the pastor situated himself in front of the pulpit. He was going to get what was coming to him now. Demetrius figured that the pastor would take one look at him and then preach a fire and brimstone message that would drive out the devil himself.

But the pastor looked out at the congregation and said, "I need y'all to pray for me this morning Saints. Because I'm struggling with the message that must be delivered today...I'm struggling because I know how true it is. You see Saints, I've been saved now for twenty years and I still war against my flesh every day so that I can please God."

Demetrius was shocked that a man of God would stand before his congregation and admit something like that. Aren't pastor's supposed to be perfect? For sure, he thought this cat was one of those guys who read his bible all day long and then used it to beat his congregation over the head with it.

Pastor Marks opened his bible to the seventh chapter of Romans, he glanced at the people and then began reading, beginning with the fourteenth verse...

For we know that the law is spiritual, but I am carnal, sold under sin. For what I am doing, I do not understand. For what I will to do, that I do not practice; but what I hate, that I do. If then, I do what I

27

will not to do, I agree with the law that it is good. But now, it is no longer I who do it, but sin that dwells in me."

Wait, what? Demetrius was truly shocked at what he was hearing. Could those words truly be in the bible. He glanced down at Angel's open bible and read the same thing the pastor had just read. Demetrius scratch the top of his head. He'd always thought that Christians were supposed to have a ready made answer for everything. And that once they accepted Christ into their lives they did not sin. Angel certainly didn't sin. His wife lived to make God proud. But maybe there were just a bunch of bad seeds in this world, who could not do right even though they greatly desired it. Isn't that what this preacher and the bible itself was saying…that men like him don't change? He was about to tap Angel on the shoulder and ask her about it, but the preacher continued reading.

For I know that in me (that is, in my flesh) nothing good dwells; for to will is present with me, but how to perform what is good I do not find. For the good that I will to do, I do not do; but the evil I will not to do, that I practice. Now if I do what I will not to do, it is no longer I who do it, but sin that dwells in me. I find then a law, that evil is present with me the one who wills to do good.

Demetrius squirmed in his seat as the pastor read that last passage. He'd come to church with his wife this morning because he wanted to be a better man. His wife had suffered long with him and he truly thought that if he stepped into the house of God that he would suddenly be different… and become the kind of man that Angel deserved. But what if he could never become that man? What if he was forever doomed to be the son of a kingpin? What if there was no way out for Demetrius Shepherd?

The preacher continued reading, now at the twentieth verse: *For I delight in the law of God according to the inward man. But I see another law in my members, warring against the law of my mind, and bringing me into captivity to the law of sin which is in my members. O wretched man that I am! Who will deliver me from this body of death?*

As the pastor finished reading from the scripture, Demetrius received an urgent text from Al. The man rarely texted, let alone sent an urgent text. He whispered in Angel's ear. "I'll be right back."

"Where are you going?

"Al is calling. This might be important so I can't just ignore him."

Angel didn't say another word. She just nodded as she turned her head toward the pulpit and continued listening to her pastor preach the word of God.

Demetrius stepped outside the church and called Al. "So, a brother can't even go to church with his wife without receiving urgent text messages from you, ugly mug?" Demetrius and Al had been Don's enforcer and one of his best friends since the men were teenagers coming up in the streets together. Demetrius couldn't count how many men Al had killed to keep Don safe. Now that Don was locked up, Al stayed with the organization in order to keep Demetrius safe.

"Man, it's lit out here and you up in church? Did Angel conk you over the head and drag you to that joint?"

"Stop talking crazy, man. I wanted to come to church with her today. Now what do you want? Any news yet on who fire bombed us?"

"Not yet. But we've got other issues."

"Lay it out for me."

"First, ten grand is missing from the money we need to send to our associates."

Demetrius sucked in his teeth. Moe had told him that the door to the storage room had been wide open when he drove back there to get the money. Dee had not been in the store and he hadn't been home, so Demetrius knew where his money was. "I'll cover it. I'm just glad we didn't loose any more than that."

"The next one isn't so easy," Al told him, then added, "The DEA just hit a dozen trap houses. They rounded up three of the top dope boys in the city… all of which get product from the house."

The House was code for the fulfillment center they used to package and ship out their drugs. "So what you thinking?"

"I'm thinking we got a mess on our hands. Just one canary could sink our entire operation."

"Al, we can't kill three dudes just because the DEA has them in custody." Demetrius wasn't for all the killing that his dad authorized while he ran the family business. But when pushed, if it meant keeping his family safe and staying out of prison, Demetrius would kill a hundred men and then sit down at the table with his family and enjoy his dinner.

"We need to keep an eye on which ones get their get out of jail free card. That's gon' be our canary. And I'm telling you now, he ain't making that court date."

"Good idea. And we don't take meetings with nobody until the heat dies down." Demetrius hung up, but as he headed back into the church, the scripture the pastor had just read rang so true to him...

But I see another law in my members, warring against the law of my mind, and bringing me into captivity to the law of sin which is in my members. O wretched man that I am! Who will deliver me from this body of death?

His wife was a saint, but he was a sinner. The worst kind of sinner, because he was a man who would always be forced to do things to protect his family that would never be Christ-like.

Demetrius put a hand on the sanctuary door, but he couldn't open it. How could he go back inside the church and sit next to his wife as if he had not just okayed the death of the man who would dare snitch on his organization. He had enough fear of God to recognize that some things would never be okay. That he would never measure up.

He leaned against the wall and watched as the preacher finished his message and the people stood. He saw Angel looking for him as the preacher asked for all who hungered and thirst for righteousness to come down to the altar. Demetrius waved at her. Angel turned back around and lowered her head. Demetrius knew that she was praying for him, and that simple fact was like a knife twisting in his heart. *Oh wretched man that I am...*

4

"This is bull, DeMarcus. I'm not going to let you play me like I'm nothing. Believe me when I tell you I'm not that girl," Jasmine Lopez told him with hands on her hips.

"I'm not trying to play you...how can I play someone who knew the deal from day one?" DeMarcus didn't know how he and Jasmine had gotten here. He was now in his second year of professional football. Running the ball and having the time of his life. The women he met knew that he wasn't trying to settle down...why should he?

"You knew I didn't want a baby. You told me you were on the pill, so how did this happen?"

Jasmine folded her arms over her chest and pouted. "Oh, now I've got to give you a lesson on how babies are made?"

"I know how it happened, I'm just not sure why it happened. Especially since I wore protection and you claimed you were on the pill. So, how could both forms of protection be faulty?"

"I didn't exactly take the pill every day like I was supposed to. There's been a lot going on lately and I kept forgetting."

"I didn't forget to cover up, so that baby can't be mine." First thing his daddy told him when he left for college was 'don't be no baby's daddy. Keep yourself covered at all times. That way you'll keep your family in one house.'

The conversation with DeMarcus' mother had gone a whole lot different. His mother made him promise to stay pure before God and find a nice woman to marry. He hadn't been able to keep his promise to his mother, but he'd never forgotten what his father had said. When he got ready to have children, DeMarcus wanted them by one woman…preferably not named Jasmine.

"You need to stop tripping, DeMarcus. You're the only man I've been with for the last six months so this baby is yours and you are either going to pay big child support or you're going to marry me and handle your business like a man."

"I'll see you when it's time for the DNA test. I'm out." DeMarcus headed for the door, wanting to get out of there as fast as his feet would carry him. He wanted to act like he was on that football field with the ball in his hand, his head down and just run.

Jasmine's hands went to her hips, she snarled at him, "How dare you. I have been good to you and I'm not going to be brushed off like I was some one night stand."

She might not have been a one night stand, but DeMarcus never saw himself staying with Jasmine for any long lasting relationship. "I don't have time for this. You got the wrong one babe. I don't roll like this."

"You're not going anywhere." She jumped up and pushed him as he walked toward the door. DeMarcus laughed at her and Jasmine slapped him.

"Don't do that again. You wouldn't like it if I struck back," DeMarcus told her.

"I bet you'd love to beat on me. All you football players are animals."

"Well, this animal doesn't put his hands on women." DeMarcus shook his head. Jasmine was beautiful, fun and carefree. The first

33

day he met her, she sauntered up to him and whispered, 'you are the sexiest man in this room, you know that, don't you?' She was the kind of woman his mother would have begged him to stay away from. And that, in a nutshell had been what kept DeMarcus intrigued. He would have never brought Jasmine home with him, but he had planned to keep her around for as long as she was willing to stay. But, the way she was talking to him now... he wanted no parts of her. "You just played yourself, Jasmine. It's over."

"You can't quit me. Not when I'm pregnant with your baby."

"I don't have time for these games. Call me when the baby is born and I'll take a DNA test." DeMarcus stormed out of her apartment silently praying that the baby she carried was not his because he did not want to deal with a manipulating woman like that for the rest of his life.

DeMarcus had no time to deal with Jasmine's foolishness. He had to get to the arena for practice. The starting running back broke his hand in last weeks game so DeMarcus was finally getting his shot and he planned to keep that starting line-up spot even after the other running back's hand healed.

DeMarcus sprinted around the field, warming his body up before doing the grueling work-out the coach had planned for him. Everything was riding on how he did in Sunday's game so once DeMarcus finished his sprint, he pushed that non-sense with Jasmine out of his mind and focused on the drills.

"I see you, rook." The starting quarterback gave DeMarcus a thumbs up as he passed by.

DeMarcus wanted to remind the man that he was no longer a rookie. This was his second year...the year he was going to make some noise. But he let it go because DeMarcus knew that actions spoke louder than words.

So he went to the weight room and did some side planks, he did his kettle bell lateral lunges as if he was getting ready to run a marathon. DeMarcus punished his body with chain push-ups and uphill speed ladder climbs. He was a man on a mission. Come Sunday he was going to show the world that he was ready for primetime.

As he grabbed his gym bag and readied himself to leave, one of the security guards tapped him on the shoulder. DeMarcus turned to face the man.

"I need you to come with me."

"I'm heading out. Can this wait until tomorrow?" Even as he asked if it could wait, DeMarcus was a bit curious. Security didn't tap players on the shoulder, they normally kept their distance and protected them from angry and/or overly enthusiastic fans.

The guard shook his hands. "It's out of my hands. The police are waiting for you."

With brows furrowed, DeMarcus asked, "What would the police want with me?"

"We need to discuss a domestic violence charge that has been filed against you."

DeMarcus swung around as two plain clothes police officers headed his way. One of them was swinging a pair of handcuffs. The other was grinning as if arresting a pro-athletic was going to be the best part of his day. "I have never put my hands on a woman in my life."

"That's not what Ms. Jasmine Lopez said. And by the look of her face, I'd say this wasn't the first time you beat up on a woman," the detective said, sneering at DeMarcus.

"When was she beaten? Because I've been here all day?"

"Let's talk about this down at the station." The detective pulled out a pair of handcuffs as he added, "If you come willingly, we won't have to use these."

"Let's go," DeMarcus stomped out of the building, all the while wishing he had never met Jasmine. The girl was mad sexy, with that Kardashian booty. But Jasmine had some kind of screw loose.

~~~

"How am I supposed to tell Angel that our son is being held at the police station?"

Al shook his head. "The good thing is he hasn't been formally charged and it hasn't hit the news yet."

"How did you hear about it?" Demetrius knew that Al had eyes and ears in several cities, but he wasn't aware that he had any contacts in Florida.

"DeMarcus called me when he got to the police station. He wanted me to tell you what was going on. Sounded like he was worried about disappointing you."

"Good looking out, but that boy could never disappoint me. He's probably disappointed in himself, though. Because he's supposed to start in Sunday's game. I don't want anything getting in his way."

"I already contacted our attorney. He's working on hiring an attorney in Tampa. DeMarcus will have representation by this evening."

"Sounds good." Demetrius stood and grabbed his keys. "Hopefully, this can be resolved before I have to tell his mama anything."

"Hold on, Demetrius. We have more to discuss."

Demetrius shook his head. "I have to get Dontae to baseball practice, so I don't have time for business right now. Remember, I do have a family and they want me to spend time with them." Plus, he was getting really tired of being head of this family business.

The look on Angel's face when she realized he wasn't going down to the altar and giving his life to Jesus nearly broke him. She didn't understand all the pressure he was under daily. It was one thing after another and no matter how much he might crave one ounce of the peace she had in her heart, Demetrius didn't see how he could ever get to that place...not as long as he was the head of a criminal empire. Some days he wished he could take his family and run. But the Columbians weren't having that. They had already assured him that they would kill him and his family if he didn't do as he was told. So, Demetrius kept showing up at work and moving product. But he didn't have to take care of this stuff at home and certainly not when it was time for baseball.

"It's Dee. He almost got himself arrested again."

What in the world was wrong with his son? "Dee just got himself home. I still need to speak to him about my money."

"If that boy wasn't a track star, he'd be behind bars right now."

"I'm listening."

"If Dee stole our money like you believe, he's using it to get into the dope business."

Head pounding, Demetrius rubbed his temples.

"He went on the East side trying to make a deal with that riff-raff, Day-Day Brown. And the boy walked right in the middle of a sting operation that Day-Day had set up with the feds so he could reduce the prison sentence they 'bout to lay on him."

"Al, are you telling me that two of my sons are looking at prison time?"

Al shook his head. "I'm not saying that. Dee, somehow got smart and never touched the package that Day-Day was trying to sell him.

So, when the police rolled up on them, Dee was already walking away."

"Dee is a Shepherd. If it even looked like he was trying to do a drug deal, the feds will be on us in no time." Demetrius couldn't believe that his son could be so stupid as to put his family in jeopardy like this.

"My sources tell me that Dee ran off so fast that the officer couldn't catch him and that Day-Day played it like he didn't know who Dee was. Which is good for him because I'd like nothing better than to cut that little weasel's tongue out."

"If Day-Day was trying to set fools up, why wouldn't he tell the police about Dee?"

"I'm sure that's exactly what Day-Day planned to do. But once my informant came on the scene he realized that giving out that info would be detrimental to his health."

Demetrius stood and paced the floor. Smoke was coming out of his ears "I have worked so hard to keep this family safe and to keep my sons out of the business my father so willingly pulled me into. And now you come in here and tell me that my son is doing exactly what I've tried to steer him away from."

"None of us encouraged Dee to do this," Al assured him. "I would have knocked him on his butt if I had caught him out there. But you gotta face reality. Your daddy's blood is running all through your kids veins. One of them was bound to go street." Al laughed at his statement, but then quickly straightened his face.

"Yeah well, when I get through with him, Dee is gon' wish he never heard of the streets. I thought the boy was stealing from me so he could go on a shopping spree, but this little ninja is trying to come up. I got a come up for him." Demetrius picked up his cell phone and punched in Dee's number. When his son answered he barked, "Where are you? Did you leave the house again?"

"I didn't go nowhere. I'm upstairs, why you trippin?"

"Get your narrow behind down here. I'm in my office." Demetrius hung up.

Within a minute, Dee opened the door and leaned against the wall. He had on a wife-beater with loose fitting jeans and prison style cornrows. Demetrius faced the facts. His son was a thug.

Dee was only 5'10 so at 6'2 Demetrius had a distinctive advantage on his son and he used it now as he towered over him. "Explain why I'm hearing things I don't want to hear?"

Dee didn't cower. He smirked, "First, you need to tell me what you're talking about."

"Where's my money?"

"What money?" Dee got this dumb look on his face like he didn't know nothin' about nothin'.

Demetrius never wanted to deal with his kids the way his father dealt with him. But Dee was the exception to the rule. Thugs needed to be dealt with. He grabbed his son by the throat and threw him against the wall. With gnashing teeth Demetrius said, "Al, tell Dee what you just told me while I choke him out." As Demetrius proceeded to choke his son out, he told Dee, "When you wake up, I expect you to get my money and put it in my hands. Got me?"

Al began informing Dee what they knew of his adventures in the dope game, Demetrius kept the pressure on his son's throat. Not once did Al say, 'come on man, stop, your son can't breathe' as Dee squirmed and tried to get out of his father's grip. The two of them acted as if this was the normal way meetings should be conducted.

"Demetrius! Demetrius!" Angel's voice could be heard in the distance as she ran toward his office. He released his son. Dee grabbed hold of his throat and slunk to the ground, Demetrius opened his door and stepped out of the office.

"I'm busy in my office, hon. What's going on?" He closed his office door.

She rounded the corner carrying Dodi in her arms. Angel's eyes were wide with fear. "Something's wrong. I can't wake her up."

5

Saul surveyed his handy work. A legion of angels had been called to battle to stop a dictator from destroying the earth. The battle had been long, but the victory belonged to the Lord as he and the other warrior angels dispatched a multitude of imps.

Saul sheathed his sword and was then immediately transported from the earthly realm into the heavens, standing not far from the rainbow that surrounded the throne like an emerald. The One who sat on the throne of grace was majestic and regal.

Falling to his knees in reverence to his Lord, Saul looked round about the throne to see four and twenty seats: and upon the seats he saw four and twenty elders sitting, clothed in white raiment; and they had on their heads crowns of gold.

From the throne proceeded thundering and lightning and voices: and there were seven lamps of fire burning before the throne, which are the seven Spirits of God. And before the throne there was a sea of glass like unto crystal: and in the midst of the throne, and round about the throne, were four beasts full of eyes before and behind. The first beast was like a lion, and the second beast like a calf, and the third beast had a face as a man, and the fourth beast was like a flying eagle. The four beasts each had six wings about them; and they were full of eyes within: and they rest not day or night, saying

Holy, Holy, Holy, Lord God Almighty, which was and is, and is to come.

Saul was granted a moment in time to glorify his Lord just as everyone else in heaven does, then he was transported into another room where he stood before Captain Aaron. Saul bowed low, "It is good to see you, Captain."

"Good to see you too, young Saul. You have done exceedingly above all that the Lord has required of you. But this next assignment will be the most difficult."

Saul put his hand on his mighty sword, a sword that had fought and won many battles. "I am at your service, Captain. Whatever and wherever you need me to be to fight for our Lord, it is my honor."

Captain Aaron told him, "The wicked one has been granted access to the Shepherd family. If he succeeds then the child could very well be destroyed and never walk into his destiny."

"Will there be an attack on Dam?" Saul remembered the last time the evil one tried to take Dam out. It didn't go so well for the enemy and his imps when they kidnapped Dam. He would make sure they felt the length of his sword once again.

"Demetrius' heart is softening towards God. But the evil one doesn't want to let him go just yet. The Lord has granted him access to all that Demetrius has, in order to see if Demetrius will finally fall on his knees and serve God as Angel has been praying, or if he will forever live in darkness."

~~~

Angel sat in her baby-girl's hospital room watching as Dodi took slow even breaths. She was resting comfortably after having her stomach pumped. The doctor discovered small traces of fentanyl in her system, then informed her and Demetrius that she would be reporting this to children services.

Demetrius ranted and raved, practically dared the doctor to do her job. But Angel took another approach, believing that killing 'em with kindness was a better approach than just flat out killing 'em. "I understand that you need to report this matter to the authorities. And we will be here waiting to speak with them because my husband and I would never do anything to harm our children...nothing."

"Thank you for understanding, Mrs. Shepherd." The doctor didn't look at Demetrius. "Someone will be here to speak with you in an hour or two. But we will not be able to release your little girl to you unless children services give the okay."

"What?!" Demetrius exploded. "You and nobody else is going to stop me from taking my daughter home, you can best believe that."

Angel's hand touched Demetrius' shoulder. "My husband and I love our daughter very much, Dr. Ames. You send in whoever needs to speak with us, and I'll turn this matter over to God." Angel kept rubbing Demetrius shoulder as she finished. "Dodi will come home with us, where she belongs."

Demetrius' phone rang. He stepped outside of the room to answer the call. Dr. Ames then told Angel, "Dodi was lucky this time, Mrs. Shepherd. But if you want to keep her safe, I suggest you make sure that no one is bringing drugs into your home."

Angel did not walk around with blinders on. She knew what her husband did for a living. But no way did she think for a moment that he would ever bring drugs into their home. But if this woman knew her current situation, she wouldn't believe a word Angel had to say, so she just nodded as the doctor walked out of the room.

Angel stood next to the hospital bed where her precious child lay. She thought about how her heart ached when she discovered Dodi on the floor, non-responsive. She was so thankful that the paramedics knew what to do for Dodi. Those men kept her baby alive and if it was the last thing Angel did, she would find a way to thank them.

A tear trickled down Angel's face as she thought of how happy she and Demetrius were when they discovered that she was pregnant. They had even named the baby Dodi because it meant 'well loved'. How could these people think that she and Demetrius would do anything to their well-loved child?

"We need to talk, Angel. Come over here with me, please," Demetrius said as he came back into the room.

Angel swung around and put her hand to her chest. She'd been so lost in thought about Dodi that she hadn't heard her husband re-enter the room. "You nearly caused my heart to beat right out of my chest."

"I didn't mean to scare you, bae. I'm sorry about that. Truth be told, I'm sorry about so many things." He pointed toward Dodi as he shook his head. "And this thing with our little girl having drugs in her system…"

As Demetrius' voice trailed off, he lowered his head in shame. Angel rushed to her husband and put her arms around him. "You didn't do this to Dodi. Don't you stand there and blame yourself."

"How can I not."

"Because you'll be feeding into the enemies hands. We are under a spiritual attack and we need to stay prayed up to get through this."

Demetrius didn't have any understanding of spiritual attacks. But he knew the hand of man when he saw it. So as they sat down together Demetrius told her, "We've got trouble, bae. Right now stuff is coming at us from every direction. I need to be honest with you about some things because I don't have much time. I'm about to get on a plane and head to Tampa."

Angel's eyes crossed as she tried to get her brain to register what she just heard. "You can't leave town now. Dodi is in the hospital and we are about to be investigated by children services."

He put Angel's hand in his. "I wish I had more time to sugar coat all of this for you, but we're out of time. DeMarcus is in trouble. The police are giving him twenty-four hours to turn himself in because the domestic assault charge they questioned him about has now been escalated to a rape charge."

Angel's hands went to her mouth. She wanted to scream but she was in the hospital and her baby was in bed trying to rest after almost dying and having her stomach pumped.

"Al sent an attorney to represent him yesterday when he was only being questioned. But they think they have enough evidence to book him now."

"How could they think that DeMarcus is capable of raping anyone? He wouldn't do that." Even though Angel was convinced of her son's innocence, tears drifted down her face. It seemed to Angel that she'd cried a lifetime of tears and yet she always had more at the ready.

"Of course DeMarcus is innocent. That's why I have to get down there and get to the bottom of this mess. Believe me I don't want to leave you here to deal with everything that's going on with Dodi, but we can't let these people ruin DeMarcus' life."

"What's this domestic violence thing about?"

"The woman claims that DeMarcus beat her. This is why I know it's a set-up, because why wouldn't she tell the police about being raped at the same time she reported this so-called beating?"

Wiping her tears, Angel nodded. "You go, Demetrius. Help our son. I'll take care of Dodi."

"There's something else you need to know." Demetrius looked his wife in the eyes and broke it down to her. "First I want to assure you that I have never brought any drugs into our home. I wouldn't do that to you and the kids."

Waving that notion away, Angel told him, "That goes without saying. I know you, Demetrius Shepherd."

"I'm glad that you have trust in me like that, hon. But you need to know that Dee is trying to get into the business. I can't explain all of this right now, but—"

"Why not? Don't I have just as much right to know what's going on with our son as you do?"

"Yeah, you do. But this is not the place for that discussion."

Anger crept up Angel's spine. She loved her husband, but love wasn't always enough. She pointed toward Dodi's bed. "You may not be responsible for what Dodi is going through but you are 100% to blame for whatever Dee has gotten himself into."

Her words cut even as Demetrius tried to ignore them and get to the task at hand. He put a finger to his lips, leaned closer to Angel and whispered in her ear. "I have cleaners at the house right now. If Dee has any drugs in the house the people I hired will find them and dispose of them."

Angel whispered in her husband's ear. "You think Dodi got into something that Dee stashed in the house?"

"I don't know, but we will discuss it more once I get back in town, okay?"

"You leave me with this bomb shell and then just say, 'we'll take about it later. But you and I know that later never comes."

Demetrius didn't respond, he just stood as he prepared to leave. "Call our attorney and let him deal with children services if you run into problems."

46

Angel wanted nothing more than to continue this conversation and get to the bottom of what happened to Dodi and what in the world was going on with Dee. But she knew her husband well enough to know that he would simply refuse to answer any more questions.

Demetrius bent down and kissed Angel. "I love you, bae. I'll get back as soon as I can."

Angel dearly loved her husband. She and Demetrius had endured their share of ups and downs. She trusted him, even though he was always so secretive with her. But what Angel didn't understand was why Demetrius even told her as much as he did, so she asked, "What made you tell me this?"

He glanced back at her and answered honestly, "After all you've been through with me, I just couldn't bear it if you thought I had done this to our child...I'm trying to change, Angel. And I truly want to prove that to you."

This was the man she fell in love with. The man she'd spent years praying for. She stood up, planted a kiss on her husband's lips hugged him tight and said, "Go with God my love. I don't know what happened at church on Sunday. Because one minute you were really enjoying the service and the next, you totally disconnected, but I want you to promise me that you will leave your heart open to God."

"God don't want nothing to do with a man like me, honey. I'm just grateful that you still love me." he kissed her on the forehead. "Your love is enough for me, bae."

"Oh, how wrong you are, my love." Watching her husband walk away, Angel prayed that God would open Demetrius' heart and his eyes to the truth. Demetrius was the love of her life, had been that way since the day she met him. At one time, he was her only

protector, but then Angel learned to lean on God and trust His unchanging hand.

She desperately, wanted Demetrius to learn to lean and depend on God just as she has done. What her family was dealing with right now, Angel wouldn't wish on her worse enemy. In all the years that she had been trusting her God, He hadn't failed her yet. DeMarcus was going to be alright, Dee was going to get it together and serve the Lord rather than the evil one who ruled the streets and Dodi was going to heal from this unfortunate episode, without any lasting effects on her mind or body, in Jesus name.

Lifting her hands to her Lord and savior Angel sang a song of praise to the lover of her soul. This was how she did battle. She was waging war on the enemy right here and right now. He couldn't have not one member of the Shepherd family and she was willing to go to war to settle the matter.

6

For the first time in Don Shepherd's adult life, he was nervous. He'd turned seventy-one last week, but Don wasn't sure how many more days he had on earth if he remained behind these prison walls. He and his best friend...his brother, Stan Michael's had both received a ten-year sentence for drug trafficking. The prosecutor had dropped the murder charges they'd tried to pin on their organization. Don and Stan took the deal so they could walk out of prison instead of dying of old age on a life sentence. This was the year of Don and Stan's release.

Never in a million years would Don have thought his heart would be cut out of his chest with the death of his best friend. He and Stan had grown up together, ruled the streets together, built an empire together and went down together. Their ten years were almost up and Don thought for sure that he and Stan would walk out of this joint and start handling business again.

But Stan had collapsed one night after dinner. He was then rushed to the infirmary. That was the last time Don saw his friend alive. They told Don that Stan died of a heart attack, but Don wanted to see some proof of that. Seventy wasn't nothing but a number, Stan still lifted weights every day, jogged around the block and stayed away from fried chicken and gravy, so they could go head on with that heart attack mess. Once he was back on the street, Don was determined to get to the bottom of the matter.

Desperate to get from behind these walls, Don had even considered praying, but a man like him could never receive help from God...especially because of what he intended to do once he figured out who set the death trap for Stan.

He might not be able to get a prayer through, but Don did know someone who could. His very own grandson, Dam had some kind of hotline to the man upstairs. Don was going to make sure that Dam got him a fair and speedy hearing in the highest court of all.

"Guards...guards."

One of the guards came running as if Don paid his salary rather than the federal correctional institution. And in fact, the correctional institution did pay the guard every two weeks like clockwork. But it was that unmarked envelope that he received once a month that kept him driving his most adored Land Rover and his wife in her Lexus ES 300. "What can I do for Mr. Shepherd?"

"I need to make a phone call."

The guard unlocked the cell and walked Don through the block. On their way to the phone, a man in the cell closest to the doors yelled out. "How you gon' take him out of here when I been begging one of y'all to take me to the infirmary."

"Ain't nothing wrong with you," the guard shouted at him. "Sit down and wait until somebody comes to get you."

"Man, this ain't right. Y'all be favoring these old heads over us all the time. Last month you took that other old head to the infirmary before me and y'all know I needed my inhaler."

The old-head this young cat was referring to was Stan. Don turned cold penetrating eyes on the young thug. He snarled, "Boy, do you want to die tonight?" He might have been put away for ten years, but Don wasn't about to take this kind of disrespect.

"I got this Don. Don't waste your breath on this punk." The guard pulled the pepper spray off his duty belt and sprayed the young prisoner. "Now I said sit down and wait your turn."

The boy backed away, coughing and gasping for air. As the guard opened the door and took Don to the pay phones he said, "Sorry about that stupid kid. I know Stan's death hit you hard."

Don nodded. "Stan was like a brother to me."

The guard stepped back, giving Don space to make his call. Dontae answered the phone, Don would have loved to hear Dee on the other end of the line. Al had told him what his wayward grandson was up to and Don didn't like it at all.

"Hey Dontae, my man, what you been up to?"

"Nothing much, Pop-Pop. Just playing baseball."

"Yeah? Your dad must have signed you up for that."

"Yep. Dad says I'm going pro."

Don had few regrets about the way he lived his life. But one thing he did regret was that he didn't give Demetrius a fighting chance to stay in baseball after his injury. "Watch how you slide into those bases. Don't want to end your career before it begins."

"I'll be careful Pop-Pop. Sure wish you were here so you could come to my games. Mom and Dad are way too busy right now."

That didn't sound like Angel and Demetrius. They were always at the kids activities. "Oh yeah, what's going on with them?"

"Dodi is in the hospital. Mom couldn't wake her up the other day. And Dad left town to go check on DeMarcus."

Don hadn't talked to Al in about three days, so he wasn't up on anything that was going on with the family. He'd give Al a call in a minute, but he had to know one thing, "What happened to Dodi?"

"She got real sick yesterday and that's all I know."

He'd ask Al about Dodi too. "Okay, can you put Dam on the phone for me?"

"Yeah, sure." Dontae put the phone down and then yelled through the house. "Dam, come get the phone, it's Pop-Pop."

When Dam picked up, Don couldn't do nothing but smile. Dam had a special place in his heart because at just three years old the kid warned him of a plot against his life. Don was alive today, because of his grandson. Now he needed Dam to get right back on that hotline and tell God to set him free. "Hey my man, how's it crack-a-lackin'?"

Dam laughed, "You talk funny, Pop-Pop."

"Well you're only ten, I guess you don't have much cracking... going on."

"I was just praying for Dodi. She's sick."

"I heard. I want you to keep praying for Dodi, but I need you to add Pop-Pop to your prayers too."

"Okay, Pop-Pop."

"This is serious, Dam. Pop-Pop needs to get out of this prison." Don didn't feel safe behind the walls after how Stan went down. It was only a matter of time before they got to him. "I need you to ask your God for a favor for me."

"Got it. I'll do it right now, Pop-Pop."

Don called Al as soon as he hung up with Dam. Al ran down everything to him. It saddened Don to discover that his family was falling apart. He needed to be on the outside so he could squash this attack that seemed laser focused on the Shepherds. His parole hearing wasn't for another two months, but Don needed to get from behind these walls much sooner than that.

~~~

"Boy, what have you gotten yourself into?" Demetrius demanded of his son as they sat on the back patio watching the Florida palm trees sway.

DeMarcus looked as if he'd just had the worse night of his life. He hadn't shaved and his eyes were blood shot red. "Dad, I promise I wasn't doing anything but hanging with that girl. She was the one who approached me in the club asking for my number…so how she gon' act like I had to take it from her."

"We'll definitely fight those claims. But what about the bruises on her face?"

"I didn't touch that girl." DeMarcus lifted his hands. "I promise dad, I wouldn't do that."

"Have you been drinking?"

DeMarcus hung his head. "I was wiped out when I got home from the police station last night and I sat up for hours, drinking and trying to figure out how I was going to restore my good name and my career."

"You're one of the best running backs in the game, your career isn't over. Your team isn't going to release you for this."

"You think not? I was supposed to start in Sunday's game, but coach called and said that I'm out until I get my situation sorted out."

Demetrius didn't like the sound of that. His son lived and breathed for the game. All DeMarcus ever wanted to be was a football player. No way was Demetrius going to allow DeMarcus' dreams to be crushed like this. "Al and I are going to pay her a visit before you turn yourself in. We'll see if she sticks to her story or if she has a change of heart."

"Dad, I know how you and Al roll. I'm not judging you, but you need to know something else. Jasmine is pregnant."

Demetrius leaned over and popped DeMarcus upside the head. "Boy, what did I tell you about dealing with these females?"

Putting his hand against the spot he'd just been popped in, DeMarcus said, "I did do what you told me. And Jasmine claimed that she was on the pill too. So, there shouldn't be no baby."

"Alright son, you hang out here while Al and I check out a few things." Demetrius stood and stretched his legs, then told DeMarcus, "Don't drink anything else. I need you clear headed for what's about to go down."

"Do you think I'm going to prison over this?"

Demetrius eyed his son. "You didn't do it, right?"

"I swear, Dad. That ain't me."

"I got you. Don't worry about it." Demetrius left the house to go handle business.

~~~

As Demetrius got in the car, Al told him, "While you were inside with the kid I got a lead on somebody that I want to introduce you to."

"Let's do it," Demetrius said as they drove to the other side of town. They got out of the car and went inside the two level condo where two of Al's men awaited them. First thing Demetrius thought when he walked into the small condo, was that there was no basement so Al wasn't up to his usual tricks. That thought quickly changed when he followed Al to the bedroom and saw a man strung up by his arms with a rope that connected to the ceiling fan. "Who is this dude?"

Al pointed at the guy. "This here is DeMarcus' get out of jail free card." Al then picked up a baseball bat that was on the floor by the dresser. He walked over to the man and put the baseball bat to his head. "Now I'm only going to ask you this once and then I'm going to start swinging, you got me, my man?"

The dude shook his head so hard the ceiling fan shook.

Al then turned back to Demetrius and said, "Friends of ours found a few videos of this fool beating up women who then later went out and got restraining orders against their ex."

"So, you're telling me that women pay good money for a butt whoopin'?" Demetrius had seen and heard a lot in his life, but nothing like this.

"They sure do." Al put the bat against the man's head again. "Don't they, Danny-boy?"

"Yessss, but I don't go around beating up on women because I like it. They pay me."

"And you film the beatings?" Demetrius asked.

"Only so I can advertise my work. I got bills too."

"We don't care nothing about your bills," Al barked at Danny. "We want to know about Jasmine Lopez."

"Jasmine who?" He had a puzzled look on his face, which with his arms extended in the air with that rope, made him look all the more ridiculous.

Al swung the bat across his chest. They heard his ribs crack. Al was about to swing again, but Danny started hollering.

"Okay, okay. I didn't know her name when I did the job. But I just saw her on the news, crying about how this football player beat her up...yeah, yeah, I did it."

"Do you have footage of the beat down you put on Ms. Jasmine Lopez?" Demetrius wanted to know.

"She didn't want me to record it, but I did it anyway."

"Good, good Danny-boy." Demetrius ordered Al to untie Danny and put him in a chair. Once that occurred, Demetrius asked, "Are you comfortable?"

Danny rubbed at his wrists. "Yeah, thanks for taking the ropes off, I thought I was about to pass out."

"You complaining? Cause I can string you back up." Al told him.

"Naw, Al. I've got something else for Danny to do." Demetrius stared at Danny with cold deadly eyes. "You do want to help us out, right?"

7

As Angel waited on the nurse to bring the release papers so Dodi could be signed out of the hospital, her best friend KeKe came into the room. "Hey, I didn't know you were coming out here this morning."

"I wasn't," KeKe told her. "I had an appointment this morning, but it got cancelled so I decided to bring this to my little god-daughter." KeKe handed Dodi a balloon that said, 'Get Well Soon'.

"Thank you, Auntie KeKe."

"You're welcome baby. How are you feeling this morning."

"Much better, Auntie. I'm ready to go home now."

"Yes," Angel told her friend. "We're waiting for her release paperwork now. And trust me, I'll be happy to get home so I can take a nap...you can't get a good night's sleep in a hospital. They constantly come in and out of the room all night long, taking vitals."

"If you want me to babysit this little munchkin while you take a nap, I'm available. I certainly don't mind using my day off to look after Dodi."

Angel was grateful for KeKe's friendship. She might just take her up on the babysitting offer so she could get a quick nap. Not just because of how tired she was, but because she knew how lonely KeKe had been since her last child left for college last year. But before she could decide how she would spend the day a young woman walked into the room and changed everything for Angel.

Right away, Angel figured that this was the social worker that the doctor told her would be visiting from children services. Angel stood up and shook the woman's hand.

"Good morning Mrs. Shepherd. My name is Diane Lewis. I am the Children Services representative assigned to your daughter."

"Good morning to you," Angel greeted. "Dodi is awake and very much alert this morning. She's been talking my head off." Angel offered the woman a seat, but before she sat down she walked over to Dodi's bed.

She shook Dodi's hand. "I'm Mrs. Lewis, and I hear that you are one lucky little girl."

Dodi giggled. "My mom says I'm blessed and highly favored of God."

Mrs. Lewis didn't respond to that, instead she asked, "How are things at home, Dodi?"

"Good," Dodi answered then shifted her eyes toward Angel.

"You don't have to look to your mom for answers, honey. You can tell me whatever is on your mind. I'm here for you," Mrs. Lewis told her.

Dodi smiled. "Okay."

"No, wait. Are you insinuating that I would instruct my daughter to lie to you?" Angel tried her best to be respectful of others in all situations, but she was not going to let this woman falsely accuse her.

"What's going on here? These people don't think you tried to hurt Dodi, do they?" KeKe asked, confusion showing on her face.

"You heard her, didn't you? This is unbelievable. You can't come in here and throw around unfounded accusations like this." Angel wasn't going to let this happen.

Before Diane could respond a man strutted into the room as if he had every right to be there. He had on regular clothes, but he showed Angel a badge. "I'm Detective Green and right now you have two choices. You can either sit down and let Mrs. Lewis do her job or you can step outside the room until we call you back in."

"Oh, so now you think you can come in here and talk to me all kinds of craziness too. Well, I'm calling my attorney. I am Dodi's mother. I take excellent care of my child and I'm not going to be bullied by anyone about my child." She picked up her cell phone and dialed their attorney, just as Demetrius had instructed her to do.

After she explained everything to her attorney he asked to speak with the detective. Angel reached her arm out to hand him the phone. "He wants to speak with you."

"Ma'am, I am not obligated to speak with your attorney. I'm here to help Mrs. Lewis."

Angel put the phone back to her ear. "He won't take the phone."

"Put me on speaker," he told Angel. She did as she was requested and her attorney spoke loud and clear. "My name is Harold Brown, and I have already won three successful cases against children services for not following lawful procedures while dealing with minors and I have won two cases against the police force for misconduct. So, I suggest that both of you back out of that hospital room until I get there so that this interview of Dodi, who is my client as of this minute, will be conducted correctly."

"We can't leave Mrs. Shepherd alone with the child. That might contaminate the investigation." Diane's voice rose ever so slightly.

"Then don't leave, but don't speak to my client until I arrive. I can be there within fifteen minutes. Will that work for you?"

"Yes, I guess that will have to do," Diane said as she and the detective took a seat.

Dodi's bottom lip quivered. Angel kissed her on the forehead. "I love you, honey. Everything is going to be alright. I don't want you to worry, okay?"

"Okay mommy. I love you too."

"I'm going to step out for a minute to call your daddy. I'm not going anywhere, I'll be right by the door."

"Are you sure?"

"Positive. I'll even let you speak with your dad before we hang up." Angel turned to KeKe and asked, "Can you stay in here and watch Dodi, for me?"

"Of course I can. Give Demetrius a call. I'll be right here." KeKe sat down in the chair next to Dodi's bed.

Angel stepped just outside the door so that she could hear if either Mrs. Lewis or Detective Green said anything to Dodi. She called Demetrius and waited for him to pick up.

Before she could tell him what she was dealing with, he joyfully asked, "Did you catch the morning news?"

"No, I've been too busy to watch the news."

"You might want to turn it on, because DeMarcus is being vindicated as we speak."

Angel wanted to rush back into Dodi's room and turn on the television. But she wasn't about to watch it with her current guests around. "Tell me what happened."

"Long story short, Jasmine hired this dude to beat her up so that she could frame DeMarcus with the crime. But the guy who did the job filmed it. The news stations are showing his handy work now."

"How did they get the tape?" she asked, then quickly said, "Never mind, I'm just thankful DeMarcus is off the hook." Angel figured that Demetrius had something to do with the news stations receiving that video...her man was a fixer, she desperately needed him to fix her current situation.

But then Demetrius went on to explain, "He's only in the clear on the domestic violence charge so far. But now that the police know that she lied about DeMarcus beating her, I'm sure they will drop all charges soon enough, and then we can celebrate."

"Why wouldn't they just drop the whole thing. This girl is obviously a vindictive liar?"

"The girl is gone. The police can't find her and neither could I. And believe me, I looked high and low for her."

"You think she left town after the footage of her beating was shown on TV?" Angel was confused. She didn't understand how any of this could be happening to her first or last born child.

"She's Columbian, so she might have left the country to avoid answering questions about her false report. I'm sure she figured that before it's all over, she would be the one behind bars."

"Better her than DeMarcus." Now it was time for Angel to rain on Demetrius' parade. "A children services representative showed up this morning with the police. They tried to get me to leave the room so they could question Dodi without me."

"Did you do what I told you?"

"Yes, our attorney is on the way right now. I will call you back once I'm done with these people."

"Sounds good, baby. I'll get myself on the next plane and be home before nightfall."

61

"Thank you." Angel's voice was shaky. Tears ran down her face as she leaned against the wall. "Thank you for what you did for DeMarcus and for coming home. I need you here with me."

"Baby, please don't cry. I will be back home today. Just let our attorney handle everything."

"Okay." She wiped the tears from her face. "Dodi wants to talk to you." Angel went back into her daughter's room and handed the phone to Dodi."

"Daddy, is that you?"

"Yes honey, it's daddy. How's my princess doing today?"

"I feel much better. But where are you, Daddy? Mommy is so sad here without you?"

Angel took the phone from Dodi. "That's enough talking for now, Dodi. You rest for a few minutes and then I'll let you talk to Mrs. Lewis again, okay?"

Dodi twisted her lip and put her arms across her chest. "I don't want to talk to her."

Angel didn't want Dodi to talk to her either, but she didn't see how they had much of a choice. As she hung up with Demetrius Angel did what she always did when she didn't know what else to do, she prayed. She didn't care that others were in the room. She opened her mouth and called out to her God. Lifting holy hands, Angel called upon the Lord to, "Deliver us O Lord, from the hands of the enemy. Protect us O Lord. Don't allow the enemy to win this fight. Help us Jesus...I'm calling on You, because You knew about this attack before it ever hit us. My family is falling apart, but I trust You Lord. I trust You to bring us out and lift us up. Jesus! Jesus! Jesus!

~~~

In his spiritual form, Saul was so tall that no human could stand eye to eye with him. But, whenever he presented himself in his earthly form Saul made sure to stand at least a foot shorter than Shaquille O'Neal. People still stared at him but he was always able to point to someone else who was taller than himself, at least in his earthly form.

He got off the elevator on the third floor where the parole board was housed. Saul was holding a briefcase with only one set of forms in it. He waited patiently as the clerk helped others in line. When it was his turn, he stepped up to her, opened his briefcase and handed her the forms.

"My goodness, you're tall," she said as she took the forms out of his hand.

"I get that all the time. But at least I'm not the tallest man on the planet." He pointed to his forms, then flashed his pearly white teeth. "Those need to be processed asap if possible. I'm kind of late with them."

The woman didn't understand why she was grinning back at this extraordinarily tall man, nor why she decided to close her station down to log the information on the forms into her computer. She might have been confused about her actions, but she was happy none-the-less that she could help this man out.

8

"Hey Shepherd, you need to hit the shower. You've got a parole hearing scheduled today."

"What are you talking about?" Don asked the guard as he unlocked his cell. "The only hearing I have scheduled is in two months."

"I don't know, maybe your hearing got expedited because you are scheduled to be transported to the courthouse today."

Well, well, well, Don thought to himself. His grandson had a serious hotline to heaven. Don gladly left his cell and did as he was told each step of the way towards his freedom.

Within a matter of hours Don was seated in front of a five-panel parole board. Three white men, a white woman and a latino man. Hardly a jury of his peers, but Don was ready to roll with it. He was coming from behind the walls and he didn't care if he had to beg, bribe or lie to do it.

"Mr. Shepherd, it is our understanding that you made a deal with the feds that allowed you to come up for parole review at the ten year mark."

Don looked at the white man, who appeared to be sitting on his high horse, thinking he could keep him behind the walls and that Don could do nothing about it. Giving the man a gentle smile, Don said, "That is what I was told, sir. I've kept my nose clean and I've tried to follow the rules of the prison system each and every day I've been there."

The latino man abruptly interrupted with, "What about the guy who was murdered a couple of cells away from where you are housed?"

Don's eyes bucked as his brow arched, "Sir?"

Looking at his paperwork, the latino man said, "This happened about six and a half years ago. Several inmate statements said that the man tried to kill you during the night and by morning he was found dead."

"None of those statements said, I had anything to do with that man's death, right?"

While all the men started flipping pages, reviewing their notes and other documents, the white woman said, "There has been one complaint turned in against you, Mr. Shepherd. One of the inmates thinks that the guards show favoritism towards you. Why do you think this inmate believes such a thing?"

Don slightly slanted his head as if he was thinking about the question asked of him, but in actuality, he was wondering what kind of slow death he would provide for that whiny kid. "I think I know who you're referring to. Mike Little, he has asthma and he gets upset when the guards don't take him to the infirmary when he requests it. He also hasn't been there that long. So, he hasn't seen how I have developed a good rapport with the guards because of the way I follow their rules and encourage other inmates to do the same."

"Uh huh," the white man with wire rim glasses smirked as he continued the assault. "And what about your criminal activities outside of prison? Are we expected to believe that you are a changed man and you'll just go and work at a Wal-Mart somewhere if we release you."

"Sir, in case you haven't noticed, I'm an old man now. I won't deny that I lived a very wild life and even participated in criminal activities. But I've done my time for all of it. All I want to do now is go home and hang out with my grandkids."

"We did receive a letter from the warden, expressing your years of good behavior and his confidence of your rehabilitation," the final man on the board stated.

Money well spent, Don mused.

"Your daughter-in-law also wrote a letter stating how you and she have developed a better relationship. She also discussed your grandchildren and how much they love and miss having you in their lives."

"I miss them too. Believe me, I have learned my lesson. Being behind bars and not being able to watch those precious grandbabies grow up has been the hardest thing I've ever had to endure. So, I promise you all, that if you approve my parole, you will never see me in here again." Don didn't promise to go legit, he couldn't lie that good. But he was sure of one thing, he would never allow himself to be taken alive again.

"Thank you, Mr. Shepherd. We will review all of our information and provide you with an answer in the next few days."

~~~

When Attorney Harold Brown arrived, he informed Diane Lewis that he would be recording the interview. Mrs. Lewis then went back over to Dodi's bed and resumed her line of questioning. Angel still didn't like the questions, but her attorney was able to squash some of the inappropriate questioning.

When the interrogation was over, Angel thought they would just leave them alone and that she would be able to take Dodi home. But once the release papers were signed, Angel was informed that Dodi would be released in the custody of children services.

"This is outrageous. Dodi answered all of your questions. She has not been mistreated in our home. We love our daughter."

"I don't doubt that you love your daughter, Mrs. Shepherd. But I wouldn't be doing my job if I let Dodi go home with you without doing a complete home study first."

"What does that mean?" Angel turned from Mrs. Lewis to Attorney Harold Brown.

KeKe put a hand on Angel's shoulder trying to calm her.

Attorney Brown said, "This is routine procedure. Someone from children services will come to the house and talk with you and your husband. They'll want to see where Dodi sleeps and get a general impression of what home life is like for her."

"That's fine, but why can't Dodi come home with us? I don't want my child in some foster care situation."

Attorney Brown turned to Mrs. Lewis and said, "The Shepherd's are loving parents, who have provided a suitable home for their child for all of her life. Not only that, but they have raised four other children who haven't been in any trouble."

Angel thought about what Demetrius told her about Dee and what DeMarcus was currently dealing with, but she still nodded in agreement. She had good kids and she and Demetrius were good parents. Nobody was going to take that away from them.

"Even if all that is true, the child could have died. So, we can't just turn a blind eye to this." Mrs. Lewis pointed toward the detective. "Detective Green and I will take Dodi and then we will be in touch with you to set up visitation and the home study."

Angel screamed, "No!"

Attorney Brown asked Angel, "Do you have a family member who can take custody of Dodi?"

Angel was distraught and crying, but she wiped her eyes as she thought for a moment. "My mother would take her, but she doesn't live here."

"Would she be willing to move here until we can sort this situation out?" Attorney Brown asked.

"Yes, I'm sure she would. My mother would do anything for my children." Maxine Barnes had been her rock when Dam was first born and she and Demetrius couldn't see eye to eye. But her mother stepped in and allowed Dam to live with her while Angel and Demetrius sorted things out.

"Since your mother would be coming from out of town she will have to be approved by the court," Mrs. Lewis told her.

Angel felt a headache coming on. She paced the floor as she rubbed her temples. They were trying to take her daughter away from her. She lifted her eyes upward. "God in heaven, do You see what is happening. I need you Lord."

"Don't forget about me, Angel. I am now a licensed foster care provider."

Angel's hand went to her mouth. "Oh my goodness, that's right. KeKe had such a big heart, but an empty nest, so she had decided to open her home for other children who might be in need. Well, Dodi was in need now.

"What about it, Mrs. Lewis? Will you allow Mrs. Shepherd's friend to take the child until we can make other arrangements?" Attorney Brown asked.

"If her paperwork is in order, I don't see why not," Diane stated.

Angel shouted hallelujah! But in the same moment, Dodi started crying. Angel went to her daughter and hugged her. "Calm down baby, we are going to sort this out."

"I'm sorry I disobeyed you mommy." Dodi was sobbing now.

"You didn't disobey me. You didn't do anything wrong."

"Y…yes, I… I did. I ate too much candy and now I'm sick just like you told me."

Angel was confused, but nothing was new there. The events of this week were sending her in a tailspin that she didn't know how to get out of. But one thing she knew for certain was that she had not given Dodi any candy. She was very strict about the amount of sugar her children had in their system. So, she never brought candy home. "Where did you get candy from, Dodi? Please tell Mommy what you're talking about."

"The nice lady at school gave it to me."

"What nice lady? Did your teacher give you some candy," Angel doubted that, because Dodi's teacher knew how Angel felt about sugar.

"No." Dodi shook her head. "This nice lady who came to the school for grandparent's day gave it to me. She told me not to eat too much at one time, but it was so good that I ate three pieces and now I'm sick."

Angel swung around to Mrs. Lewis. "Did you hear my daughter? Someone gave her candy. That might be how she ended up with traces of drugs in her system. Why don't you go find that woman instead of harassing us?"

Attorney Brown lifted up his recorder. "We've got it all on tape so I'm sure the detective will go to the school and find this mysterious woman who came to the school on grandparent's day."

The detective stepped forward and asked Dodi, "Do you have any more of the candy this nice lady gave you?"

Dodi didn't answer him, she turned her face to the wall.

Angel said, "This is important Dodi. Can you tell me where the candy is?"

Dodi turned back to her mom. "Are you mad at me?"

"No, baby, I'm not mad. We just want to figure out why you got so sick. If that candy is making kids sick, you don't want anyone else to eat it, do you?"

"No Mommy, I don't want anyone else to get sick." Dodi leaned over and hugged Angel and then said, "I hid it in my jacket pocket so you wouldn't find it."

9

Angel was still thanking God that KeKe had been able to take Dodi home with her. She served a God who was more than able to calm the raging storm. Things were not perfect, but Angel trusted KeKe and knew that Dodi would be in good hands.

She went home with Detective Green and located Dodi's jacket. Angel tried not to think too much about the fact that Dodi was not allowed to sleep in her own bed as she entered her child's bedroom. She was on auto pilot as she went into Dodi's closet and grabbed the coat off the hanger.

She was about to reach into the pockets but Detective Green stopped her. "Let me do it." He pulled on a pair of latex gloves and then searched all of the pockets on the jacket until he found the bag of candy in the inside pocket. "She's a good little hider."

Despite the situation, Angel smiled. "She knows I don't want them eating candy."

As they headed back down the spiral staircase toward the front door, Detective Green asked, "Don't you have other kids at home besides Dodi?"

"Three of my sons, still live at home," Angel answered not certain why the detective asked.

But then he said, "I'm surprised that your home is so clean. You've been at the hospital for two days and nothing seems out of place in your home. My boys would have spaghetti hanging from the ceiling."

"Mine would have normally done the same, but they know this is a stressful time for me, so I guess they're giving me a break." Angel was not about to tell this man that her husband hired cleaners. That would only make him suspicious and they had no reason to suspect her family of anything.

Angel opened the front door as she asked, "How long will it take to have that candy analyzed?"

"Shouldn't take more than a few days. I'll get back to you as soon as I know something."

"Thank you for checking into this. I greatly appreciate what you are doing for Dodi."

Once the detective left, Angel packed a suitcase for Dodi and sped over to KeKe's house where Diane Lewis and her attorney were waiting. KeKe signed the papers to accept Dodi into her home.

Angel and KeKe hugged. "I don't know how to thank you, girl."

"Thank me for what? We're family and this is what we do. I still remember how you and Demetrius took me in and helped me get on my feet so that I could get my kids back when they had been in the system." They hugged again, then KeKe told her, "I'm praying for you. God is going to move the mountain for you and your family."

"I don't care what you say. I will be thanking you until the day I die for this one, KeKe. If you hadn't been able to help my baby I probably would have lost my mind worrying about her."

Angel handed Dodi a coloring book and some crayons. "Go sit down in the kitchen and color for a little while sweetheart."

"Okay Mommy." Dodi skipped all the way to the kitchen table and then sat down with her coloring book as if this was just an ordinary visit with Auntie KeKe. Angel stayed with Dodi and KeKe for a couple of hours after Mrs. Lewis and Attorney Brown left. She fixed Dodi a sandwich and tried to act like everything was fine. But time was running out for Angel. She would have to leave soon in order to pick the boys up from school.

Before she left, Detective Green stopped by KeKe's house with a few pictures for Dodi to look at. He told Angel, "After I dropped the candy off at the precinct I stopped by Dodi's school to check things out."

"And?"

"And Dodi was right about that grandparent's day thing. So, I printed off the pictures of everyone who signed in that day. We have about twenty pictures and I'd like to see if Dodi recognizes anyone."

"Great, thank you," Angel said as she and KeKe watched Dodi look at each photo that Detective Green handed her. She didn't recognize anyone at first. But Dodi gave a double take at the ninth picture handed to her.

"That's the lady who gave me the candy."

"Are you sure about that, Dodi?" Detective Green asked.

"Yes, yes. She was really nice to me."

The detective then left, promising to call her with any information he discovered. Angel thought Detective Green was on his job, purely for the sake of doing what was right, until he said to her, "Make sure you tell your husband that I'm taking care of this."

Angel side-eyed the man, wondering why on earth he wanted her to deliver a message to her husband after the way he tried to treat her at the hospital. But then she reminded herself of how helpful he had been since Dodi mentioned the candy and agreed to do just that.

After the detective left, Angel glanced at her watch. "I've got to get going. Don't want to be late picking up the kids."

73

KeKe popped some popcorn and told Dodi, "We're going to watch movies tonight. You've probably already seen every movie I have, but we'll have fun with them anyway."

"Yay! I love popcorn and movies."

"And I'm going to order us a pizza too. How about that?"

Angel loved that KeKe was trying to make this fun for Dodi... just like a sleepover with pizza and popcorn. Nothing like a child that had been ripped out of the arms of her mother and placed with a family she didn't know. "Demetrius should be home in a few hours. I'll come back and spend the night with her."

KeKe shook her head. "Children services could remove her from my house if you did that while they're still investigating you."

Tears sprang to Angel's eyes. "But my baby has never spent a night away from me."

"I'll Facetime you a couple of times tonight and then you'll come back and hang out with us tomorrow. It will be okay, Angel. I promise you."

Angel wanted to pick her daughter up and run away with her. But where could she run. Things were getting real complicated. She left KeKe's house and then cried all the way down the street. She picked up the kids and then ordered pizza when she got home because she didn't feel like cooking and she thought it would be a nice distraction for the boys just as it was for Dodi.

When Demetrius arrived home, Angel ran to him and threw herself in his arms. She desperately needed to know that life would one day soon go back to the way it was. But for now she would have to be content finding safety in the arms of her husband and her Lord and Savior. "I'm so glad that you're home. I'm not doing to good right now."

Demetrius took his wife by the hand and lead her to the sofa in the family room. "Your eyes are bloodshot, bae. You've been crying all day, haven't you?"

"I just can't believe this." Angel sat down next to her husband. "They have taken our child and we haven't done anything wrong."

"KeKe came to the rescue once again, even after how badly I treated her for so many years." Demetrius shook his head unable to fathom how someone could continue to do good for others even while receiving very little thanks for the effort.

"KeKe has been a Godsend in our life. I used to think that she was placed in our life so that we could help her. But it has always been the other way around. She is my spiritual sister and I love her like we were blood sisters."

"I still wished they would have let Dodi come home. This is where she belongs, not over at Auntie KeKe's house."

"I feel the same way. But the system has put us on trial. Every question that social worker asked Dodi was geared towards you and I and what we might have done to cause that drug being in her system.

"They were grilling her like that and Attorney Brown didn't stop them?" Demetrius was getting so angry it seemed as if smoke was coming out of his ears.

"Attorney Brown kept her in check for the most part, but since Dodi did have drugs in her system he had to allow most of the questions. I'm just so thankful that he was recording the whole thing because I doubt if they would have even looked into this candy situation if it hadn't been recorded."

Demetrius sat up. "I got your message about the candy. But I'm not understanding who gave it to her. Was it one of the teachers?"

"No, it wasn't a teacher. Some lady who signed in at the front office. She was supposedly visiting a kid for grandparent's day. But somehow ended up giving Dodi this bag of candy. We will know for sure if the candy was laced with fentanyl in a few days. But we have a bigger problem."

"What can be bigger than what happened to Dodi?"

Angel told him, "The police don't know who this woman is. They pulled the school records of everyone who signed into school three days ago. Detective Green showed the pictures to Dodi, she picked the woman. But the name on her driver's license is a fake."

"You know what this means, don't you?"

"No, Demetrius. I don't understand any of this. And I certainly can't understand why some woman would give our child something that could have killed her."

"That's the whole point. Someone is trying to destroy our family." Running his hand over his head, Demetrius stood in front of the fireplace. His head hung low. When he turned back to face his wife he said, "It's no coincidence that two women who've tried to hurt our kids are suddenly ghost. Someone is orchestrating this nightmare. But I promise you, Angel. If it's the last thing I do on earth, I will protect this family."

"Well, everyone is in for the night, so hopefully nothing else will go wrong. I just want to Facetime my baby and then go to sleep." Angel headed upstairs to say goodnight to her boys, and that's when she noticed that Dee had left the house. She tried to reach him on his cell phone, but of course he didn't respond.

"If that's the way you wants to play it, then fine," Angel muttered. Her son was eighteen now, so if he didn't want to listen to them, Angel realized that it was time to pack Dee's things and let him go. She would have to trust God to take care of her wayward son, because she was no longer going to allow him to live in her home and run the streets rather than do something productive with his life. Like college or getting a job.

~~~

Dee had planned to lay low, watch a few movies and then go to bed. With all the drama going on with Dodi he didn't want his mom worrying about anything else tonight. But then he received a text that he couldn't ignore.

Dee had been making moves on this hottie for weeks. She kept playing hard to get, talking 'bout she had a man and wasn't looking for another. But Dee wasn't having that, because after all, he was a Shepherd. And what a Shepherd wanted, he got.

The girl's name was Leann Jones. She was about 5'7 with an hour glass figure. She was a Paula Patton look-a-like with a Kim Kardashian booty and Dee had to have her. "I've been dreaming about you all week," he told her as he stood at her front door.

Twirling her long black hair, Leann said, "I've been thinking about you too. I'm glad you were able to come over tonight."

Dee's hand was on the door jam. "So, you gon' let me in or what."

Leann stepped back and let Dee enter her apartment. His eyes scanned the room. A big, plush sofa sat directly in front of the fireplace. Big bold statues of inanimate objects were placed throughout the room. African American art hung on the walls. "I thought you worked at the Sprint store?"

"I do."

Pointing around the room, Dee asked, "How you living like this?"

"I told you I had a man and that he was good to me."

"If he's good like this, then why you got me up in here?"

With pouty lips, Leann told him, "I thought my man loved me. But he's been acting funny lately...like he's ready to move on. So, if he's leaving, I've got to look out for myself, right?"

Sounded good to Dee. Sounded even better when Leann invited him to spend the night. Dee didn't ask himself why this woman was suddenly interested in him or why she was willing to sleep with him before he even bothered to take her out to dinner, he just went with it. By morning when he woke Dee put his arms behind his head and stretched out in Leann's king sized bed, he was feeling really good.

Leann wasn't in the bed, but as he called out to her, she walked back into the bedroom carrying a breakfast tray. "I figured you were hungry, so I made you an omelet."

Sitting up in bed, Dee was all smiles as he looked at the plate she sat in front of him. Omelet, link sausages and a fruit cup. As he sliced into his omelet and took a bite, Dee knew without a doubt that he had to figure out a way to keep Leann in his life. "Girl, you trying to make me move in here or what?"

Her eyes beamed. "I would love for you to move in with me, Dee. But as you can see, I have expensive taste."

"I can see that." If he had been able to make that deal with Day-Day, Dee would be making money right now. But Day-Day had been playing games, and he almost caught a case dealing with that fool.

"Do you think you could take care of a girl like me? Would your dad hook you up so you can get rolling?"

"My dad would sooner see me holding a 'I-Work-For-Food sign before he'd hook me up. The man pretends like he makes his money from that strip mall, when everybody knows that mall is just a front."

"So, how do you make money? Or do you just live off your daddy?"

"Oh I've got money, believe that." Dee might have stolen his bundle from his dad, but he wasn't going to let that get in his way.

Leann took the fork out of Dee's hand and started feeding him. As Dee chewed his food, Leann said, "So, do you want to be with me, baby?"

Dee's head bobbed.

She fed him again. "You know, I have a cousin who could help us flip some money."

"I've got some things in the works." He really didn't, but Dee couldn't let Leann know that he didn't have a plan. He'd probably have to drive over to Cincinnati so his dad wouldn't get wind of what he was doing. Dee could make something work.

"I heard that you almost got arrested trying to buy cocaine from Day-Day."

"How'd you know about that."

"Word gets around." She was smiling at him as she picked up the fruit cup. "You want some?"

"No, I'm full." Dee pushed the tray back and got out of bed. Everyone seemed to know about what went down with him and Day-Day. Dee was feeling like his first big score had turned into an epic failure. His dad probably thought he was an idiot.

"We really should talk with my cousin, baby."

"What's this 'we' stuff?"

"I've put aside a little money. If you can go in with me we can get enough weed to make some real money."

10

When Angel woke up the next morning she hurriedly got Dam and Dontae ready for school . Demetrius put a few toys for Dodi in his SUV and headed over to KeKe's house while Angel dropped the boys off. She normally prayed for God's hedge of protection over her children every morning just before letting them out of the car, but this morning, Angel's mind was on Dodi and the investigation that brought her parenting skills into question. So, it was not until she had already drove off that Angel realized she forgot to pray.

"Get it together, girl. Don't fall apart here." Yes, there was a lot going on with DeMarcus, Dee and Dodi, but Angel couldn't forget about her other two children. She looked to heaven and prayed, "Help me, Lord. I can't function without You."

Demetrius was already parked at KeKe's house when she arrived, and for a moment that irritated her. Why did she have to drop the boys off so Demetrius could get over here and see Dodi before her? "Stop being petty." She was talking to herself a lot these days. Trying to encourage herself to stay calm even when she wanted to scream.

When she walked inside the house, Demetrius joked, "It sure took you long enough."

Angel nudged Demetrius' shoulder. "You could have dropped the boys off at school and I would have gotten here a lot sooner."

"You know something," he admitted, "I didn't even think about taking that load off of you."

Angel picked up Dodi and gave her a kiss. "It would have been nice, especially this morning."

"Okay babe, you're right." He looked at his watch. "Tell you what I'll do. I have a couple of meetings today, but once I'm finished I will picked the boys up from school so you can hang out here with Dodi. How does that sound?"

"You'll feed them too?"

"McDonalds for err' body." Demetrius laughed at his own joke.

Angel gave her husband a kiss. "Thank you, baby." His simple gesture put a smile on her face. Her husband was paying attention to her, understanding her limits and Angel appreciated that. She sat down next to him and took comfort in the arm he put around her shoulder.

"How much longer do you think we'll have to do this?" Demetrius asked her.

"I don't know, bae. I'm just praying that the candy has traces of that fentanyl in it and that the police finally believe that we didn't do anything to Dodi."

"What about the woman who gave Dodi the candy? Are the police even trying to find her?"

"I don't know, but Detective Green told me to tell you that he is taking care of everything."

"Is that name supposed to mean something to me?"

Angel shrugged. "I'm just telling you what the man said."

Demetrius kissed Angel, then said, "Oh, I forgot to tell you…my dad met with the parole board early, so if his parole gets approved, he might be getting out any day now."

"Oh my God, that is great news." Angel pulled her husband's face toward her and kissed him again. "Now we can get on with our lives and move away from this town."

Demetrius shook his head. "Not so fast, honey. I don't know what my dad is going to require of me or for that matter what our business associates might require."

Angel got quiet as she silently prayed for Demetrius. She needed for this nightmare to be over. She was so tired of having armed guards protect their home, and watching her back everywhere she went, tired of her husband being beholden to evil doers rather than God. *Please, Lord, help my husband learn to put his trust in You.*

"I've got to get going," Demetrius told her, then turned to his daughter, "but before I do…" his words trailed off as he picked Dodi up and swung her around.

"Swing me again, Daddy…swing me again."

Demetrius obliged. Then he sat Dodi on Angel's lap and planted a kiss on her forehead.

"Okay hon, I'll see you at home later," Angel said.

After Demetrius left, Angel and KeKe hung out watching television and catching up on each other's lives. KeKe had taken the week off from work so she could help Angel out with Dodi. But she received a call from the restaurant with an issue that she had to take care of.

KeKe told Angel, "I'm sorry, girl, but I've got to get to the restaurant. This might take a few hours because our supplier has messed up our order."

"It's fine, KeKe. Go take care of business. Dodi and I will be here when you get back."

"Okay, but we've got to be careful. So, don't answer the door if that social worker shows up and don't let Dodi start any fires."

Angel stood up and saluted KeKe as if she was a soldier, addressing her commander-in-chief. "Yes ma'am."

As KeKe walked out the door, Angel went into the kitchen to fix Dodi her favorite lunchtime sandwich, peanut butter and jelly. "You need anything else, honey?"

"Milk."

"How could I forget the milk?" Angel opened the fridge, filled her daughter's cup with milk and then stood and watched while Dodi ate her sandwich. Her child had eaten a PB&J sandwich at least four days a week since she was two years old. So, there was nothing new about the way Dodi ate this sandwich, but Angel still didn't want this moment to end.

She was with her child and nobody was accusing her of being a bad mother or of turning a blind eye to things that might be going on in her household…things that could hurt curious six year olds. "I brought a puzzle, do you want to work on it with me."

Dodi scrunched her nose. "I'd rather watch TV." Wiping her hands Dodi left the kitchen table and grabbed the remote.

Angel wasn't about to deny her child anything at this point, so she sat on the sofa and watched hour after hour of Dora The Explorer.

~~~

Al was waiting on Demetrius when he arrived at the office. Demetrius hung his coat on the coat rack and then sat down behind his desk. He put his briefcase on his desk and opened it just as a normal businessman would do. Demetrius longed for the day that anything would be normal about his day.

"You want the good news or the bad news first?" Al asked.

Taking some papers out of his briefcase, Demetrius admitted, "I could use some good news right about now. So, please hit me with that first."

"Your father's parole was approved. I'm driving down there today to pick him up."

"That was a quick turn around."

"Tell me about it. One day he's telling me that he met with them suits at the parole board and the next thing I know he's telling me to come pick him up."

Demetrius was trying to determine how he felt about seeing his dad again. How he felt about taking orders from Don Shepherd once again. He'd always felt like a boy, trying to be a man whenever he was with his dad, and maybe that was because Demetrius had allowed his dad to railroad him into so many things that he never wanted for his life in the first place.

"I hope you feel that I watched over you the best I could these years that Don has been gone."

Demetrius nodded. "We've had some bumps in the road recently, but in truth, I probably wouldn't be alive today if you hadn't stayed with the organization and looked after us."

Al sat down in the chair in front of Demetrius' desk. He looked troubled as he said, "Looks like we've got another bump in the road. You ready for the bad news?"

Demetrius wondered if he shouted NO and then held his hands to his ears would something like that be enough to stop the bad news from coming? "Let me get a cup of coffee first."

Demetrius went over to his coffee maker, turned it on. Waited while it dispensed hot black coffee into his cup and then sat back down. Trying to delay the news for as long as possible, Demetrius asked, "Do we have a Detective Thomas Green on the payroll?"

Al shook his head. "Not on our payroll. Why'd you ask?"

"Dude is on Dodi's case. He told Angel to tell me that he was taking care of things or something like that. Just trying to figure out what's up with that."

"Don't know, but he's the least of our worries today. You and Angel are going through a lot, so the last few days I've been having Dee followed to make sure he stayed out of trouble."

"Good looking out," Demetrius said as he took a sip of his coffee.

"It didn't help much. He was with some chick last night. He didn't leave her apartment until this morning and when he did he was in handcuffs."

Coffee sputtered out of Demetrius' mouth. "Are you kidding me?"

Al lifted a hand. "Before you get too upset with the boy, you need to know that, yes, he got caught buying weed. But the girl he was with set him up."

"Who is this girl?"

"Her name is Leann Jones. I don't know much about her yet, but trust me, I'll get to the bottom of this."

"Why do you think she set him up?" Dee could get in trouble all by himself. He didn't really need a set-up, so Demetrius was a little leery about this.

"Ten minutes after the police left, that Jones girl had her bags packed and was trying to get out of there like the place was on fire. The whole thing didn't smell right to me."

"Where she at now?"

"I had my boys take her to the basement. I'll deal with her when I get back."

Al had dubbed an abandoned house that he used to torture and beat those who got out of line, The Basement. So, Demetrius knew exactly where Ms. Leann Jones was. He also knew that things weren't going to be good for her tonight. "What's the bail amount?"

"I don't think he's been processed yet. You can probably take care of a few things around here before you go bail that boy out." Al patted Demetrius on the shoulder and then said, "I shouldn't have laughed the other day when I said that Dee was turning out to be like his grandfather. I know you don't want that."

Shaking his head, Demetrius took another sip of his coffee. No, he didn't want that, but if his son was bound and determined to be a gangster, Demetrius didn't know how he was going to stop him. He also didn't know how he was going to tell Angel.

~~~

Dodi was laughing her head off at something Dora The Explorer had just done. Meanwhile Angel was about to drift off to sleep. But as her eyelids lowered, her cell phone rang. Angel didn't recognized the number but she answered anyway. It was a collect call from Dee. She accepted. "Boy, why are you calling me from jail? Your daddy is going to hit the roof."

"Don't tell Dad about this, Mama."

"How can I avoid telling your dad that you got arrested again!"

"Daddy choked me the other day, Mama. If it wasn't for you running downstairs with Dodi, he probably would've killed me."

"Why would your daddy choke you?" Angel thought that Demetrius was too hard on Dee. But he wouldn't do something like that, not to his own son.

"It's true Mama. All because I didn't respond to him quick enough. So, what you think he'll do to me now? We both know that your husband don't like me anyway."

"My husband is your father, so address him as such." She shook her head. "If you would have stayed home last night, you wouldn't be in trouble right now. I don't know what makes you think I have time for this mess."

"Mama, please…they got me down here on bogus charges. I wasn't even doing nothing…I don't want to spend the night in this place. Can you please post bail so I can get out of here?"

Letting her son spend the night in jail, just might be the best thing for him. He was always getting into something. She had half a mind to call his dad and let him deal with Dee. But Demetrius had anger issues when it came to dealing with Dee. And at this point, she couldn't deal with the argument she and Demetrius would get into over Dee's antics, not when they had this situation with Dodi going on. "What did they arrest you for?"

"They claim I was trying to sell weed to an undercover agent. Can you believe that, Mama? As much money as we have, why would I need to sell weed?"

She didn't know why her son needed to do any of the things he did, but she believed that he'd been caught doing it. Thank God it was just weed. "I'll bail you out this time, Dee. But hear me good. If you get arrested again, I won't come running."

"This won't ever happen again, Mama. I've learned my lesson."

I thought you didn't do anything, she wanted to say. But it would be wasted breath and Angel preferred using her breath to pray for her son. "I'm on my way."

KeKe was still at the restaurant straightening out issues. KeKe was already doing enough for them, so Angel didn't want to bother her friend. She couldn't call Demetrius because he would then know something was up, and right now, she couldn't deal with the fallout from Demetrius knowing what Dee had done. So, she put Dodi's coat on, went to the bank to get the money needed for Dee's bail and then went to the courthouse.

But Angel soon discovered that she couldn't hide anything from her husband. "What are you doing here? She asked as she ran into him just as she and Dodi were getting ready to be scanned for weapons.

"So, I guess Dee called his mommy."

"Did he call you too?" Angel saw the anger in her husband's eyes. Lord knows she didn't need her husband behind bars for assault and battery for beating his son to a pulp.

"You know that boy didn't call me. He probably told you not to tell me that he was down here...that's why you didn't call me either."

He had her there. But then she realized that all though she was standing in front of her husband with Dodi by her side, she didn't see Dam and Dontae with Demetrius. "Where are the boys?"

A puzzled look crossed his face. "You didn't pick them up?"

"Of course I didn't pick them up. You said you would do that. Don't you remember offering to pick up the boys so I could spend more time with Dodi." Angel slightly raised her voice in her frustration. She kept reminding herself that she loved her husband, even as he was sorely testing her patience.

Demetrius popped his forehead with the palm of his hand. "I completely forgot about the boys after I found out about Dee."

Angel's hand was on her hip. "And just how did you find out about Dee. You just admitted that he didn't call you himself." For years, Angel had accused Demetrius of keeping the guards around the house to spy on them. But he always claimed that the guards did not monitor their comings and goings, only the comings and goings of visitors. But she didn't know if she believed him anymore.

He leaned over and whispered to her. "I've got my sources, but I'm not going to discuss it in here."

"How could I forget, you're like the FBI. Everything is top secret and no comment with you again, huh?"

"It's not like that Angel. But you need to go get the boys."

Angel consulted her watch and realized that Demetrius was right. She didn't have time to stand there and argue with him. The boys had been dismissed from school ten minutes ago. She had to get going. "Did you bring the bail money with you?"

Demetrius shook his head. "I don't carry that much cash around. I was going to talk to him first and see if I wanted to bail him out."

"Pay the bail, Demetrius." Angel took the money out of her purse and put it in her husband's hand. She then picked up Dodi and headed out the door.

But just as she was leaving the courthouse, Diane Lewis was entering. She stared at Angel, then blurted out. "What are you doing with Dodi?"

Angel turned back to her husband. "Demetrius can you talk to Mrs. Lewis, I have to pick up the boys." Angel kept walking out the door and heading toward her car. Mrs. Lewis shouted at her, "But you shouldn't have Dodi with you. I will be speaking to KeKe about this matter."

11

Dontae's high school was one block over from Dam's middle school. When no one showed up to get him, Dontae walked down to Dam's school to see if his brother had been picked up. The whole walk down to Dam's school Dontae kept thinking about the sweet ride he was going to get the moment he turned sixteen. Enough of this waiting-on-your-mama stuff.

When Dontae rounded the corner he saw Dam standing alone looking around like he was lost. Dontae figured that Dam was hoping to see that white Mercedes that normally pulled up to the school with their mom waiting inside the car to greet them with a smile. He hated to break it to his brother, but with all that was going on, their mom must have forgotten them.

He had almost reached Dam when a teacher walked up to his brother. Dontae could hear the man say, "You better come back in with me. We'll give your mother a call."

His mother was already frantic with Dodi being taken away from them. Dontae didn't want teachers thinking their mother just left them to fend for themselves. So, he sped up and grabbed hold of Dam. "Let's go. I'm sorry I'm late."

Dam turned to face his brother. "I thought Mom was picking us up?"

Dontae glanced at the teacher as he shook his head. "My brother is forgetful sometimes." Dontae pulled on Dam's shoulder. "Come on, let's go."

"But isn't he normally a car rider?" the teacher asked.

"Ah yeah," Dontae was holding onto Dam as tight as he could. No way was he going to let Dam get caught up in the system as Dodi now was. "My mom normally pick both of us up. But our baby sister is in the hospital so she asked me to walk Dam home today. We just live a couple of blocks from here."

"Okay," the teacher said, "Just make sure that you're on time tomorrow if your sister is still in the hospital."

"I will, sir." Dontae tugged on Dam's arm again and the two of them started walking.

Dam gave his older brother a questioning glance, "Why'd you lie to my teacher like that? Dodi isn't in the hospital anymore."

"I know but Mom forgot us and I didn't want her getting in any trouble."

"Mom never forgets about us. Maybe she really did ask us to walk home today and you just goofed around at your high school too long."

"Shut up, Dam. You don't know everything." Dontae got aggravated with his brother at times because he was so super smart and got straight A's all the time, so his parents were always holding Dam up as some example for the kind of grades Dontae should be bringing home. But Dontae didn't have time for all that studying, when all he wanted to do was play baseball.

"I know that you left me at school and I'm going to tell Mama when we get home."

"Tell her whatever you want, I don't care." Dontae knew he was right and he wasn't about to let his annoying little brother work his nerves.

They had about ten more blocks to go to get home, when Todd, one of the security guards who opened the gate in front of their house pulled up next to them. "Sorry I'm late boys. Hop in so I can get you home."

"But where's my mom?" Dam asked, looking like he didn't want to get into Todd's car.

"Quit asking questions and get in the car, Dam." Dontae had baseball practice in about an hour and didn't want to tire himself out walking ten more blocks when they had a ride. He opened the back door. Dam still looked skeptical, so Dontae shoved him towards the car.

Dam got in and then scooted over as Dontae got in. "Thanks for picking us up. Where's our mom?" Dontae asked.

"I'm taking you to her now. Just sit back and enjoy those snacks I picked up for you and your brother." Todd locked the doors and sped off.

~~~

Angel was frantic with worry. She had driven to both Dontae's and Dam's school and the kids were nowhere to be seen. Dam's teacher was still at the school when she arrived. The man told her that Dam's older brother walked him home. So, Angel rushed home, only to discover that Dam and Dontae were not there.

She received a call from the security booth. Angel picked it up, hoping for some news about the boys. But Dave told her, "KeKe is here. Is it okay to let her in today?"

"Yes, of course. Please let her in." Angel then asked, "Have you seen the boys?"

"No ma'am, the kids haven't been here since you left with them this morning."

Then where were her sons? What was happening? "Dave, I need you to drive around the neighborhood to see if Dontae and Dam are out there somewhere." Angel wanted to do it herself, but she needed to get Dodi back with KeKe first.

"Todd isn't here. I can go when he gets back. Is that okay?" Dave asked.

"No, Dave. I need you to go now. Don't worry about the security booth. I will let Demetrius know that I sent you to look for the boys."

"I'm on it. I'll give you a call in a minute."

"Thanks Dave." She turned around in her massive gourmet style kitchen, looking this way and that. DeMarcus was in Florida. Dee was in jail. Dodi was in the house with her. She knew where three of her children were, but something inside was telling her that Dam and Dontae weren't just on a leisurely stroll home…her boys were missing.

"Mommy, where are my brothers?" Dodi asked.

Angel held the phone for a moment, looking as if her lifeline had just been cut off. She was completely frozen, unable to think or do anything. Her family was under attack and Angel didn't know which way to turn.

The doorbell rang.

She heard the sound, but it took a moment before it registered that someone was at the door. Then she remembered KeKe had been at the gate. Angel willed her feet to move, step by step she made her way to the door and opened it for her friend.

"Why'd you leave the house with Dodi?" KeKe asked as she stepped in.

"It's been a crazy day, KeKe. First, Dee got arrested. I went to the courthouse to bail him out. Then Demetrius forgot to pick up Dam and Dontae. Now I can't find my boys anywhere."

KeKe quickly asked, "What about friends? Do you think they might be at someone's house?"

Angel thought of something and picked up the phone. She called Dontae's baseball coach to see if Dontae had shown up for practice. But Dontae's coach didn't answer so she left a message.

When Angel hung up the phone, KeKe said, "I hate to add more to the pile, but Mrs. Lewis called me. She said that if I don't have Dodi in my possession today that she was going to pick her up tonight."

"I'm sorry I took her, but I didn't have a choice. Do you think you can smooth this over for me?"

"I'll give Mrs. Lewis a call and let her know I have Dodi. Hopefully, that will chill her out."

The phone rang. Angel picked it up and Dave told her, "I don't see them. Do you want me to keep looking?"

"Please keep looking, Dave. I don't know where my boys are." She hung up with him and then called Demetrius. She thought hearing Demetrius' voice would reassure her that everything was going to be alright. But she felt even more helpless when he hung up without saying goodbye. Standing in the middle of the floor, Angel could do nothing but giggle until she buckled over. She then sat down on the floor and kept on until the giggles turned to tears.

KeKe sat down next to Angel and put her arms around her. "I know it doesn't feel like it right now, but God is going to turn this around for you."

"When KeKe? I just keep getting hit and God isn't listening, because if He was my sons would be home with me. I can't even keep my daughter, you have to take her with you." Angel felt hopeless. She didn't want to blame God for her situation, but where was He? Why wasn't He keeping her family safe as He had done for so many years?

"Don't lose hope, Angel. God loves you and he cares about the things that concern you." KeKe held onto Angel's hands. "We need to pray."

At this point, Angel was unable to say anything but, "Lord, why?"

So, KeKe took the lead and began crying out to the Lord on her friend's behalf. "We come to You now Lord, in need of help. You have taught us to trust You in years past as You have come to our aid in so many instances. We can do nothing else but to trust You even now…"

~~~

Demetrius scowled at Dee. "You're costing me money every time I turn around. You doing too much Dee. Recognize when you 'bout to be cut loose."

With defiance, Dee told him, "Look Dad, I don't know what you want from me? I come from a family of gangsters, this is all I know."

Demetrius wanted to smack his son in the mouth. But he'd been jumping on this kid since he turned sixteen. Not one beat down had changed Dee's mind, so Demetrius decided it was time to try something different. "Son, why do you think I own a strip mall?"

Leaning back in his seat like he was hiding from the po-po, Dee answered, "It's a front for your real business. You think I didn't know where all that money came from in the storage room?"

This smart mouth boy really got on his nerves sometimes. "For your info, the strip mall was supposed to be my way out of a life of crime. I never wanted to be the head of a criminal operation."

"Then why do you do it?" The look on Dee's face said, he didn't believe his father.

"You're eighteen so you're old enough to know the truth about what has really been going on in this family. So let me lay it out for you." Taking a deep breath, Demetrius continued, "It is true that my dad groomed me to be the same kind of man he is. When I was younger I didn't have a problem with it, because, what else was I going to do? My dreams of going pro were squashed when I slid wrong and broke my ankle."

"Well, you should be happy that you've got DeMarcus and Dontae interested in all of that pro sports stuff...but that's not me, dad. I'm more like you and Pop-Pop. I just don't know why you can't accept me as I am?"

"Let me finish, Dee." Demetrius didn't know if he was wasting his breath or not, but he had to try. "After I married you mom and we started having kids I realized that the street life was no way to raise a family. I wanted out so I used my dad's money to buy the strip mall."

"Ha, and you got mad at me for using your money."

"It's not like you were paying for a college education with the money, you were trying to buy drugs...now do you want to listen or not?"

Crossing his arms around his chest. "I'm listening."

"Like I was saying...I was trying to get out of this life, because I wanted you boys to be about something different. But then Don got arrested and it was then that I discovered that my father was making drug deals with the Columbians. They burned down our house and threatened to kill Don, you, your brothers and your mom if I didn't take over the business. So yes, my strip mall became a front for a drug cartel, but I only did it to keep you safe. This is not fun and games to me. This is real life, where young punks like you end up dead."

When Dee didn't respond, Demetrius tried another tactic. "Anyway, gang banging and drug dealing isn't all you know. Your mother's people are Christians…good people who don't get involved in all this street drama. Why don't you follow after them?"

"They're boring," Dee complained.

"They're in their seventies and they are still alive. The rate you're going, you might not even make your twenty-first birthday. And what do you think that would do to your mama?"

When Dee didn't respond. Demetrius reached over and punched him in the gut. "Answer me, boy? How would your mama like to see her son dead?"

"She wouldn't like it," Dee said through clinched teeth. "But I doubt that you would care much. I'm just a problem child to you."

"You know what? I'm done talking. Let me get you to the strip mall so you can start working on this bail money you owe me."

With an eye roll, Dee said, "Whatever."

Demetrius was about to give up on the talk-some-sense-into-your-kid thing and just knock Dee's teeth down his throat. But before he could make a move on his son, his cell phone rang. He saw that it was Angel so he hit the button on his steering wheel to answer. "Hey bae, Dee with me, so stop worrying. We'll be home right after I stop by my office."

"I need you home now," she shouted into the phone.

"Dee needs to work off some of that bail money. We'll be home soon enough. But it's time for this boy to recognize what time it is."

"Dontae and Dam are missing!" she blurted out.

"What? What did you say?"

"I can't find Dontae and Dam. They weren't at the school and they're not at home even though Dam's teacher told me that Dontae walked Dam home today."

"I'm on my way." Demetrius hung up. He then put in a call to Moe. "My boys are missing. Something doesn't smell right here. I need you to gather a crew and meet me at the house."

"I'm on it, Demetrius, I got your back," Moe told him.

Demetrius busted a U and headed home. "I was supposed to pick your brothers up today. If something happened to them because of your foolishness...God help you, my son."

Dee beat the back of his head on the headrest. "I'm sorry Dad. I really am. I didn't think nothing would happen to my bros."

As Demetrius pulled up next to the guard shack in front of his house, he gave Dee a hard cold stare. "This is how the game works, Dee. Always some fool out there trying to take you down...you want this?"

Demetrius didn't wait for a response from Dee. He rolled the window down and looked for the guard. He needed to tell them to let Moe and the crew in the moment they arrived, but no one was in the security booth.

12

Saul sometimes took on familiar forms in order to get the job done. Today he looked just like the sergeant of Detective Green's police unit. Saul was wide mouth chewing two sticks of gum just as the sergeant did every day. He was also carrying Dodi's candy in his hand. When he reached Detective Green's desk, he banged a fist on the man's desk just as his sergeant had done hundreds of times.

When Detective Green turned to face the man he assumed was his sergeant, Saul threw the candy on his desk. "What's this about?"

Detective Green's eyes widened. "Sergeant, where did you get that candy?"

"It was in your trash, but I don't understand why, when that children's services worker keeps calling asking if the lab results have come back on the candy that Shepherd woman gave you."

"Well I...well I."

"Stop stuttering, Green. If you think I'm going to let you occupy this desk while you pretend to do your job, you've got another thought coming."

"I am doing my job, sir."

"Then get this candy down to the lab and give that children's services worker the information she keeps calling here asking for." Saul stood at Detective Green's desk, staring at him until he got out of his seat, picked up the candy, put it in a baggy and then started walking.

Saul put a hand on Green's shoulder. "I'll walk with you. I need to go down to the lab myself." Once Saul had ensured that the candy was logged into the lab in order to be tested, Saul then went into the sergeants office, closed the door behind him and then promptly disappeared.

~~~

KeKe called Diane Lewis and let her speak to Dodi and Angel in an effort to calm the woman down. Angel was on the phone with the woman trying to explain why she had Dodi with her at the court building today when her house phone rang.

KeKe whispered, "I'll get it. You keep talking to Mrs. Lewis." Instead of picking up the receiver, KeKe hit the speaker button so that Angel would be able to hear both sides of the conversation. "Hello, Shepherd residence. Can I help you?"

"Mama, where are you? I don't want to stay here anymore."

Angel recognized Dam's voice. She dropped her cell and ran towards the kitchen phone. "Dam! Dam! Where are you?"

The front door opened and Demetrius and Dee rushed in just as Angel was hollering into the speaker.

A computerized voice took over the call. He said, "Dam doesn't know where he's at, but I do. If you want to see either of your sons again, then I need $2,250,000."

"Who are you? Why are you doing this?" Demetrius demanded as he stormed into the kitchen.

"You don't need to know who I am, you just need to get my money?"

"I will kill you, do you know that?" Pure hatred flooded through every syllable that Demetrius uttered as he hit the record button on their answering machine.

Tears ran down Angel's face as she asked, "Can I speak with my sons, please?"

"Since you are much nicer than your husband. I will put your kids back on the phone but this will be the last time you hear from them until I get my money."

There was a clicking sound and then Angel could clearly hear Dontae say. "I'm sorry I got in the car. I thought you sent him."

"Sent who, Dontae? Who picked you up?"

There was another click on the line, then the computerized voice said, "That's enough family time."

"No!" Angel screamed.

Dee put an arm around his mom. He held her up as she broke into sobs. "Please put my boys back on the phone."

"If you hurt my brothers, I will pull your guts out after my dad is done killing you. You don't know who you're messing with." Rage emboldened Dee, made him reckless with his mouth.

But Angel wasn't having it. "You shut up and go sit down somewhere," she told him as she wiped the tears from her eyes, trying to compose herself. As Dee stepped away from her, KeKe took his place and held onto Angel's hand.

Demetrius was saying, "I don't have that kind of money laying around here. You'll have to give me time to get it."

"Tomorrow at noon," the computerized voice said.

"Where?"

"I'll call you tomorrow and tell you where to drop the money." After those words the line went dead.

"This is a nightmare," Angel screamed and screamed some more.

"I'm going to get the boys back, Angel. Just trust me on this," Demetrius said. Then the door burst open. Moe came barreling through with men carrying guns and snipper type rifles.

Wide eyed, Angel turned to Demetrius. "What's going on? We need to call the police, not your boys. Just what do you think is going to happen if you go after our kids with guns a blazing?"

"I'll be in the basement. I need to talk to my boys for a minutes and then you and I can talk."

Demetrius was about to walk off with Moe and the crew but Angel grabbed a fist full of his shirt. "No! You want to meet with these guys, then we all will meet with them."

"You don't need to know any of this. Don't you get it, Angel. I have always tried to keep you out of the things I have to do to protect this family."

She let his shirt go, stepped back as she told him. "Look around, Demetrius. Your family has not been protected. So, no more secrets, no more lies. I'm tired of it." She stood there staring at him, waiting for him to make the next move. Angel wasn't sure how Demetrius was going to respond, but she was determined that from this moment forward there would be no more secrets in this family.

She had stood by her husband through thick and thin. Whatever he wanted to do, she allowed without saying anything to him, because she knew what kind of man she'd married. But he had also promise to protect this family and never allow any of his dirty dealings to affect them. But Demetrius could never keep a promise like that because he had no way of knowing who or what would be thrown at them on any given day.

Sighing deeply, Demetrius pointed towards the furniture in the living room. "Okay fellows, have a seat let's figure this out together."

KeKe followed behind Angel as she stomped up the stairs.

"I can't take any more of this. Everything is falling apart," Angel pointed a finger downstairs, "It's his fault and he won't even admit it."

"Thank you, Angel said to her husband. She then turned to KeKe. "Can you take Dodi upstairs and have her take a nap?"

As KeKe walked away with Dodi, Demetrius pointed at Dee. "You can go find something else to do too."

But Dee shook his head. Tears were in his eyes. "If it wasn't for me, my brothers would be at home. You can't shut me out, Dad. I have to help."

"Let him stay Demetrius. Having him in our sights is one less thing we have to worry about."

Demetrius snapped a finger. "Speaking of which, I haven't talked to DeMarcus since I got home. We need to get him on the line and make sure nothing else has happened to him."

"Good thinking," Moe said. "Let me call him from my phone so you and Angel can keep your line free incase this guy calls back."

While Mo was calling DeMarcus, Demetrius pointed at one of the gunmen. "I need you to man the security booth. I don't know what's going on with Dave and Todd but the booth was empty."

"I sent Dave out to look for the boys. You might want to call and tell him to come back." Angel told Demetrius.

"Even if you sent Dave out, Todd should have still been there. Is he on some kind of extended break or what?"

Angel shrugged.

"Okay, I've got DeMarcus on the phone. I'm going to put him on speaker," Moe told the group.

Angel and Demetrius said a quick hello to their son and explained to him that the boys had been kidnapped. Then Angel said,

"I know that you all don't necessarily believe the way I do things, because you think you have to fight your own battle." She directed her eyes at her husband, then continued, "But since Dontae and Dam are my sons, just as well as they are Demetrius', I'm asking that you all lock hands with me and let's go before the Lord in prayer before we figure out what to do next."

Demetrius nodded to his boys. They all got up and joined hands around the room. Angel bowed her head and prayed to her Lord and Savior. She knew that nothing she could say would stop Demetrius from doing battle the way his father had taught him...but nothing he could say would stop her from doing battle the way her father had taught her either.

~~~

"Man, if you ain't a sight for these old eyes." Al grabbed Don in a bear hug as the two laughed and rejoiced at Don's home coming. They had come up in the streets together, along with Joe-Joe and Stan. Only Al and Don were left so as Al drove Don home, the two reminisced about the good ol' days.

They had a good time laughing and joking about Joe-Joe and Stan's antics, but Don's tone soon changed as he said, "Stan's death hit me hard. I thought we were both going to walk out of that prison this year. But somebody got to him, there was nothing natural about Stan's death and we are going to get to the bottom of this."

"Something is definitely going on. The family is being attacked at every level. But I did find out something about that chick who was trying to put the screws to DeMarcus."

Don's lip tightened as he listened.

"Remember how I told you that I thought the Columbians were coming after us?"

Nodding, Don said, "Yeah, but that doesn't seem right to me because we don't owe them nothing…and business has been good."

"I had a few of my guys stay in Florida to find her. If she couldn't be found I was prepared to say she was probably back in Columbia and then I would know that we had a serious problem. But they found her hiding out at a friend's house."

"Did they take that lying gold-digger to the police?"

"Yep, but Demetrius had them give her a pregnancy test first. So, no worries, no more grand babies are on the way."

"So, she lied about the baby…typical."

"It was a shake down by a pretty little girl who was crazy enough to pay some dude to beat her up."

Don shook his head. "Man, I must have been behind the walls too long. Because I thought women didn't like to get beat."

Laughing, Al told him, "The last women I slapped, threatened to slit my throat. So, I don't have any understanding about this one. DeMarcus better quit running around with these cuckoo birds."

"Yeah, well, cuckoo bird or not, them charges better get dropped against my grandson or catching a case for lying will be the least of Ms. Lopez's worries."

"The problem we have is that the girl who got Dee arrested is not a cuckoo bird. She deliberately set him up for that arrest."

"In other words, if we figure out who was behind Dee's set up, then we'll probably find out who fire bombed the store…I guarantee you the same cat is behind that too." The wheels started turning. Don said, "Hand me your cell phone."

Al handed his phone to Don and he called his son's house. He was going to get to the bottom of this right now. On the third ring, Dee answered the phone.

"Just the man I wanted to speak to," Don said.

Dee shouted, "It's Pop-Pop," to the group. Then he said to his grandfather. "I can't talk long. We have to keep this line open."

"What's that about?" Don wasn't used to being brushed off by his grandkids.

Demetrius took the phone. "We're having a crisis right now, Dad. Someone has kidnapped Dontae and Dam."

13

Thunder roared and the heavens shook at the news that Dam Shepherd had been abducted. Satan had been allowed to wreak havoc on the Shepherd family, but the one thing Satan couldn't do anything about was the prayers that were coming up to heaven. And because of those prayers a legion of angels had been released to help Saul deal with this attack.

Forward…The legion of angels shifted the weight of their body to their right foot as their swords hung on their side, ready to slice through the nearest imp. March…They marched in formation with thirty inch steps, arms swinging in natural motion without bending the elbows like a mighty army on its way to battle.

The heavens opened and the mighty army continued to march as they descended from the place of peace, where the Godly received their reward of being with God for eternity, to the place where Satan and his imps ruined lives every second of every day.

~~~

Dontae yawned and then rolled over. He felt groggy and weird. Like his head was floating away from his body and all he wanted to do was go back to sleep. But he couldn't sleep because he needed to find Dam. This was all his fault. If he had kept walking his little brother home rather than selfishly worrying about whether or not the walk would cause him to be too tired for baseball practice, none of this would be happening.

Lifting his head, Dontae tried to focus, but the room was so dark he couldn't see anything. "Dam... Dam? Are you in here?"

When no response came, Dontae tried to stand, but his legs were too weak to hold him up, so he started crawling around the room, letting his hands search for what his eyes could not see. "Say something, Dam. Please..." Dontae touched something as his eyes were adjusting to the dark, he saw that it was a sofa. A very dirty and dingy sofa.

As he rose up on his knees, Dontae saw that Dam was laying on that sofa. He shook his brother, trying to wake him. But Dam wouldn't wake up. "Oh God...please don't be dead," Dontae screamed as he kept trying to wake Dam.

Why had he ignored Dam? He knew his brother hadn't wanted to get in Todd's car. "I'm sorry Dam...please don't be dead." Dontae sat next to his brother and sobbed his eyes out.

After about twenty minutes of non-stopped sobs, Dam rolled over as his eyes opened to darkness. "Stop crying Dontae. I'm not dead."

Dontae nearly jumped out of his skin. He turned to see his brother lifting up. "You're alive. Oh thank God."

"Of course I'm alive," Dam told him. "I was praying, and then the angels started coming. I wanted to watch them so I couldn't wake up when I first heard you calling my name."

"What angels?" Dontae was clueless as to what his brother was talking about.

"Didn't you see them?" Dam pointed up. "Heaven opened up and I saw them. It was a whole bunch of them. They were marching towards us. The angels are coming to save us, Dontae. We're going home, just wait and see."

Dontae wanted desperately to go home and see his parents again. He wanted to believe every word his little brother said. But part of him wondered if Dam was in a delusional state because of whatever drug Todd used when he knocked them out.

~~~

"Well, old friend, looks like we're about to go to war again. You got enough left in the tank for this fight?" Don asked as he and Al pulled up to Demetrius' home.

"Guns blazing, my friend…guns blazing," Al responded.

Al and Don got out of the car and went inside. Don was comforted to see that his son had included Dee and Angel in the discussion. Family business needed to be handled by family. But Mo and his crew were needed as well. Because once they discovered who was holding his grandsons he would let loose a world of hurt on them. "I'm glad we're all here," Don told them. "Putting our heads together should help us find the boys."

Demetrius hugged his father. "Glad to have you home dad. I really need help with this one."

"I got your back son, you ain't never got to worry about that."

Al's cell phone rang. He stepped into the other room to answer it. The group kept talking, going over the events of the day, trying desperately to figure out who was out to get them.

Angel turned to Demetrius and said, "Remember when Dodi was in the hospital and I told you that we were under some kind of spiritual attack."

"Yeah," Demetrius answered but the look on his face showed that he didn't get the connection.

Angel continued, "The thing is, I think the attack started with Dee and DeMarcus, not with Dodi. This whole business about DeMarcus being accused of misusing that woman and Dee trying to buy drugs...this attack is being orchestrated straight from the devil himself."

"I'm not trying to put your beliefs down or anything, hon. But I'm just not sure how that's going to help us find the boys."

"Wait a minute though," Don paced the floor, tapping his chin. He then turned back to everyone as something struck him. "Angel just might be right. I may not know anything about this spiritual stuff, but I know enough about the streets. And this thing has definitely been orchestrated by the devil...now we just need to figure out which devil."

"What do you mean?" Mo asked.

"Forget about DeMarcus. That woman who scammed him was nothing more than a gold digger. She didn't have anything to do with the Columbians."

"You think the Columbians are behind what's happening to us? Why would they do this after all this time?" Demetrius was confused by this.

Don shook his head. "No, I never thought it was the Columbians. But Al, worried that it might be them. We have kept our end of the bargain with our business associates and they have kept theirs with us."

"Plus the kidnappers are only asking for two mill and a quarter. If it was the Columbians, they'd hit us for much more than that." Demetrius added in agreement.

"Don't forget about the firebombing. Who did that if not the Columbians?" Angel wanted to know.

"That's exactly what we are going to figure out." Don walked over to the window and peaked out the curtain. "Whoever ordered that firebombing is most likely the same person who set Dee up."

Dee piped up then, "Will you please say that again for my mom and dad. I've been trying to tell them that I didn't do nothing, but they ain't trying to hear nothing I got to say."

"Shut up boy. Ain't nobody got time for your non-sense." Angel sat her son back down.

"What I say." Dee shrugged his shoulders as he looked around the room waiting for someone to clue him in.

Al came back in the room. He put his cell phone in his pocket as he asked Dee, "How much did you know about Leann Jones before you decided to partner with her on a drug deal?"

"I ain't gon' lie, Uncle Al. I didn't know much other than the girl is fine…and she's got expensive taste. I knew I had to up my game if I wanted to be with her."

Al looked to Don and said, "Leann is Leo Wilson's granddaughter and that cop who arrested you…Detective Green was one of the cops Leo kept on his payroll back in the day."

Twenty years ago Leo Wilson had run the streets of Dayton like the mac he was. Don had been on the come up during Leo's rule. But when Leo got arrested and needed to make some cash to feed his family while he did his twenty year stint, he turned to Don. And right now, Don was remembering just how he'd made an enemy out of Leo Wilson…

14

Back in the day, twenty years ago...

Don Shepherd called a meeting that night. Demetrius was still smarting over the way he had been treated, so he originally planned to skip it. But after sitting there staring into Angel's eyes, Demetrius knew he had to get out of the house. He wanted to kiss that girl so bad that he ached. But he would never let Angel know how he was feeling. He didn't want to scare her off. It was obvious that she needed someone in her corner who wasn't out to take something from her.

"Demetrius, do you want to join us over here?" Don asked his son.

No, he didn't want to join them anywhere, he wanted to be out on a baseball field hitting homers and hearing the crowd go wild as he made his way to home base. But even after all these years, his ankle still wasn't flexible enough for him to run on the baseball field without it kinking up on him. So, here he was at another one of his father's meetings and still doing nothing about the promise he made to his mother.

"It's some real serious stuff going down," Don told the group of five, who were all considered his lieutenants. "Leo Wilson and his boys have just been indicted. They wouldn't even set a bail for Leo.

So he won't be running numbers or taking bets on the fights. Business has to keep rolling though, so Leo has asked for our help."

Don Shepherd was notorious in these parts and didn't nobody even think about messing with him. Because everybody on these streets knew that Don wasn't just the meanest hustler out there, he also had a little bit of crazy in him.

Even with all Don's crazy, Leo Wilson had remained the Head Negro in Charge. Don hadn't contested that fact, because Leo had been running the streets of Dayton, ten years before Don Shepherd came on the scene. Don respected the man; but that didn't mean that Don wasn't biding his time until he could take over, and once and for all, take his rightful place. So, it surprised Demetrius that Leo had turned to his father for help in his time of need.

"Joe Frazier's and Ali's fights both take place in December. With Leo gone, we have no competition and if we play are cards right, we can make a killing." Don clasped his hands together as if feeling the money as he continued, "Leo is handing over his contacts, so we need to get busy. As we all know, the government is running us out of the number running business. They're even proposing that the lottery proceeds help fund education. Now how can we compete with that?"

"I seriously doubt that any of them educational funds will make their way to our community. But this meeting isn't about them lottery jokers, so I'll just say this...if we make the right moves and don't make no mistakes, we just might be able to retire when it's all said and done."

"Why's Leo being so generous?" Stan Michael, Don's second in command asked.

"He wants us to break him off half of the proceeds," Don answered.

113

"Even though we getting ready to do all the leg work, and risk our necks on a hot contact list that the Feds are probably watching to see who bites first?" said Al Gamer, the lieutenant who all other lieutenants feared because he could smile at you, say good morning, put a bullet in your skull and then sit down and eat your breakfast.

Don loved Al's ruthlessness, and often put him to work against his enemies. Smiling as he answered his enforcer, Don said, "Oh my friend, you know me so well. I already told Leo that we were assuming too much risk for a fifty-fifty cut. So, he has agreed to take forty percent. At this point, Leo just wants to make sure that his family will be well provided for while he does his time."

His father sounded so benevolent with his talk about providing for another man's family and giving another hustler his cut. Demetrius just couldn't believe it. "So, you're going to help Leo out?"

Don glanced over at his son. The smile he had for Al was gone. "Why wouldn't I? Leo would do the same for me if I got jammed up like that."

"That's all good and everything," Stan said, "but when are we going to put aside this penny money we raking in and get in the dope game? You already said that the government has taken over the numbers business. So, let's just give it to them, and start raking in the real bread."

"Stan has a point," Al agreed, "Crack is blowing folks mind. I never seen people get strung out on something so fast."

Don looked at his son. "What do you think?"

"It's risky," Demetrius answered. His father had always told him that dealing heroin was out of the question because he feared becoming an addict himself. Crack was different because they *weren't using a needle and putting that stuff in their veins. But it was just as lethal.*

"No risk, no reward," Stan said.

Don thought about that a moment. He nodded. "We need to become distributors to these little corner dope men out on these streets. If we sit at the top, we get most of the reward and fewer risks."

Demetrius liked the sound of that. If he was making more money, then he would be able to stock pile enough loot to get out of this town. "I'm in."

"Without a doubt," Don said as he looked at his son as if Demetrius had no choice in the matter. "We are going to own this city. But we've got to earn enough money on these two fights before we can even think about elevating our business."

"If we get too many winners there's no way that we'll have enough money to pay them all and still be able to come up the way you talking about coming up," Joe-Joe said.

"Let's cross that bridge when we get there. For right now all we need to do is collect the bets. Make sure to talk up Frazier and Ali," Don told them.

Al laughed. "You gone crazy or something, Don? Everybody knows those two are way past their prime. They must be punch drunk to even think about getting back in the ring."

"They know what we tell them. And if you say you're putting your money on Ali or Frazier, most of them will too." Don rubbed his hands together while licking his lips in anticipation. "I'm telling you, we're gon' make a killing."

"Ali used to be like a super hero to me. But after that beating he took from Larry Holmes last year, I never thought he would get back in the ring." Al shrugged as if it was no water off his back. "If he's

going to be stupid like that, I can't think of any other group of people I'd like to see get rich from it."

On December the third, the fight between Joe Frazier and hulking Floyd "Jumbo" Cummings got under way. The fight took place in Chicago, Illinois and the gang was in attendance. Demetrius, Joe-Joe and Stan were seated in the third row, down on the floor like celebrities. His dad had said he would meet them there. Demetrius assumed that Al was late getting in town and Don was waiting on him.

Joe-Joe nudged him and Demetrius turned to see his father strutting down the middle aisle with a long haired, dark skinned beauty on his arm. Don and the woman both had on floor length fur coats; his father's was black with hints of grey around the collar. The coat the woman wore was snow white, contrasting beautifully with her skin. His daddy was showing off tonight.

Demetrius was slightly annoyed by this because he had asked for an extra ticket so that he could bring Angel to the fight. But he'd been told that this was a business trip, no distractions allowed. Angel had given him the cold shoulder after he told her he would be spending the weekend in Chicago. Sometimes he didn't understand that girl at all, but that didn't stop him from longing to be near her.

Don and his lady sat in the second row directly in front of Demetrius. He leaned over and asked his daddy, "Where's Al, I thought he was coming to the fight?"

"He's holding things down at home. We'll see him when we get back."

Demetrius leaned back in his seat wondering who this woman was and why Al suddenly decided not to attend the fight. But he didn't have much time to dwell on it because the bell rang. Smokin' Joe Frazier and Floyd "Jumbo" Cummings entered the ring. This was the first time anyone had seen Joe Frazier in the ring since George Foreman pummeled him over five years ago. But this fight was going to be Joe's coming out party. Once he destroyed this opponent, he wasn't going to stop until he got his shot at the WBA heavyweight champion, Mike Weaver.

Those were Joe's plans. But Floyd "Jumbo" Cummings was a body-building bruiser, who'd taken up boxing in prison after being convicted of murder. And he wasn't about to give any mercy to the aging Frazier, who's reactions and timing were glaringly off.

In the opening round Frazier stepped into punch after punch. It wasn't hard for the audience to see and believe that Frazier's glory days were long gone. No one wanted to see the aging fighter go down like this...no one, except Don Shepherd, who had millions riding on Frazier's demise. He glanced back at his boys and smiled.

Demetrius leaned forward to say something to his dad, but that's when he noticed that Don had a hand on the woman's thigh. He nudged Joe-Joe and asked, "Who's the new squeeze?"

Joe-Joe smirked. He leaned closer to Demetrius and whispered in his ear. "That's Lisa Wilson. Leo's wife."

When all the bets were in, the fights were over and Don and his crew counted up the money. They were excited about how much loot they'd made. Leo's cut was $2,250,000 but Don needed that money to kick start the new business. So he kept the money and even kept Leo's wife. Lisa divorced Leo in a hot minute when she realized that he wouldn't be able to support her from his jail cell.

After marrying Lisa, Don realized that he really hadn't wanted her, he had just wanted to take everything Leo ever had, everything

117

that had made him great. During the ten years of their marriage, Lisa became a fall down drunk. She eventually divorced him once she realized that he would never be faithful...never show her the kind of love Leo had shown her.

From what Don heard, Lisa had tried to make things right with Leo, but he wanted nothing else to do with her. And now after all the double crossing Don had done to Leo, it seemed as if Leo was finally getting his revenge.

15

Don looked at all who were gathered before him and acknowledged what he had done. "If the girl who set Dee up is Leo's granddaughter, then it's a sure bet that Leo has orchestrated everything that's been going down because $2,250,000 is the exact amount that I cheated him out of over two decades ago."

"And now he wants his money," Moe said matter-of-factly.

"And now he wants to die," Al chimed in with the lifting of his glock.

"Okay y'all, now that we know what's going on here, we need to cover this city until one of us finds Leo or any and everything that's important to him." Don took a gun from one of the guys who came to the house with Moe. Demetrius handed his father a set of keys to the BMW that was in their four car garage and then Don strutted out of the house...places to go, people to see.

One by one they each left the house on a seek and find mission. But as Demetrius got ready to leave, Angel stopped him. "I need you to understand something."

"What is it, Bae?"

"I pray over you and our children every day. Things may not look good right now, but I trust God. So, when I tell you to go with God, I do that believing that He will protect you better than any gun ever could. Our children will come back home, Demetrius. Just stand back and watch God work this out for us."

Demetrius looked into his wife's eyes and knew that she believed every word she uttered. "I wish I had grown up in a house that was so full of faith like you did." But then he glanced at the gun in his hand and told her, "This is all I know."

Angel wasn't giving up on her children, nor her husband. She patted him on the shoulder, "Go with God, my love."

Nodding, Demetrius walked out of the house. When Dee tried to go with his father, Angel pulled him back. "Oh no you don't. You're staying right here with me."

"I need to help bring my brother's back, Mama. I can't do that staying here with you like I'm some little kid on punishment."

Demetrius was at the door now, he opened it and then turned back to his family. "Stay with your mother," he told Dee.

Dee exploded. "I know y'all blame me for what happened to Dontae and Dam. I'm trying to do something to get them back but all y'all keep doing is telling me to go sit in a corner somewhere like I'm still a little kid."

"You want to be treated like a grown up then act like one, and recognize that you ain't ready for this." Demetrius slammed the door.

Muttering to himself, Dee complained, "Talking 'bout I ain't ready...I was born ready."

KeKe came down the stairs. "Dodi just fell asleep. She looks so peaceful I kind of hate to wake her up, but we should probably be headed home."

"KeKe, you trust God, right?"

"I know too much about Him not to trust Him," KeKe answered her friend.

"Then can you just let Dodi sleep and stay here with me and Dee and help us pray for the safe return of my boys and that the truth will be discovered about what happened to Dodi. I want all of my children home, where they belong."

"Of course I can pray with you. That social worker don't scare me. She better recognize that she is dealing with children of the most high God." KeKe lifted her hands in praise.

Angel turned to her son, held out her hand. "Come pray with us."

Dee backed away. "I know you don't expect me to pray?"

"Listen to me Dee. Right now, you feel terrible about what happened to your brothers…you even feel like it was your fault, and even though I tell you with all sincerity of heart that I don't blame you…you'll never stop blaming yourself. So, why not do something to help them."

"I tried, you and dad shut me down, just as y'all always do."

"Nobody is shutting you down now, Dee. Your brothers need you. Will you help us pray for them." Angel was still holding her hand out to her son, waiting on him to make the decision to turn his problems over to the Lord.

KeKe added, "The bible tells us that wherever two or three gather in God's name, He will be in the midst of our prayers."

Angel added, "Mark 11:24 also says, 'Therefore I tell you, whatever you ask for in prayer, believe that you have received it, and it will be yours."

"You really believe that, Mama?"

"I do son, I truly believe. Will you help us get your brothers back?"

Dee took his mother's hand and bowed down to the throne of grace just as she and KeKe were doing and they prayed and prayed some more. For Angel was convinced that this battle would not be won by the might of a man's hand or his gun, but with the help of the Lord and His angels, praise the Lord.

~~~

"I need your help Lisa," Don said as he stood in the living room of his ex-wife's home.

"Why should I help you?"

He saw the look of disgust on Lisa's face and knew that he had done much to cause it. "Look baby, I know I did you wrong. You should have never gotten involved with a man like me and I never should have promised you more than I could deliver. But this is about my grandchildren. They ain't never done wrong to nobody. Leo shouldn't use them like this."

"Leo has never been cruel to children. He won't hurt them."

"He hates me, Lisa. I did some serious damage to his reputation. I can't take the chance that he won't hurt my grandkids. I've got to get them away from him."

"What if Leo wasn't the one who kidnapped them kids? What if you go off on Leo and he didn't do anything?"

"Then I give you my word that I won't kill him."

Lisa stared at Don for a long moment. She took a puff of her cigarette. "I've only spoken to Leo once since he got out of prison. He came to me with a lie so I could sign over the deed to a house we had purchased before he went away. He said he was too old to do the upkeep on all the land around the property, so he was going to sell it."

"Why do you think he was lying? And what does that place have to do with the boys?"

"Leo would never sale that place because bodies are buried on that land. And he'd end up back in prison once the land developer discovered all those bodies." Lisa wasn't finished with her story, "At

122

first I thought Leo just wanted to go way out in the country and live out the rest of his days… maybe he didn't have enough money to buy another property and he didn't want me coming after the only place he had to lay his head. But then I found out that he moved in with the woman he'd been cheating on me with just before he got sent up."

"So, is he at the house with his woman, or in the country? Which is it?"

Lisa huffed out her exasperation. "What I'm trying to tell you is that Leo isn't using the place as his residence, so that can only mean one thing…he's using it in the same manner he did before he went to prison."

Don got it. Leo was holding his grandkids in a place where he could also bury them. "Give me the address?"

She did as Don requested. But as he was leaving, she yelled after him, "Keep your word this time. If Leo didn't do this, then just leave him alone."

~~~

As Demetrius and Moe pulled up to the guard shack in front of his house, Demetrius rolled down the window and spoke to Dave. "I'm on my way out, man. I need you to keep a serious watch over my family."

"I've got it covered," Dave told him.

"No more wondering off. I don't care what Angel calls to tell you. You let her know that you can't leave."

"Got it." Dave nodded.

Moe was about to drive off when Demetrius turned back to Dave and asked, "Where is Todd?"

Shrugging his shoulders, Dave said, "Dude told me he had a quick errand to run earlier today and that he would be right back... haven't seen him since."

Demetrius leaned back in his seat as Moe drove off. He didn't have time to worry about Todd goofing off when his kids were missing. They headed to the west side of town in search of somebody...anybody, who could tell them where his sons were. But even though they were about serious business, Demetrius' mind kept flipping back to Angel telling him to go with God. He didn't get it... what did something like that even mean? Could someone 'go with God' in the same way he got in Moe's car and decided to go with him? Was this 'go with God' stuff a physical or a conscious act?

"Do you really think Leo Wilson is behind all of this? I mean, I know he ruled the streets back in the day, but that cat has got to be old as dirt by now," Moe told him.

"I trust my dad's instincts on this one. Can it really be a coincidence that the girl who set Dee up is Leo's granddaughter and the amount my daddy owes Leo is the amount the kidnapper requested."

"That does make you think," Moe agreed.

Demetrius added, "That policeman who arrested Dee used to be on Leo's payroll, and don't forget that my dad gave Leo plenty of reasons to hate the very air he breathes."

Demetrius and Moe parked the car and hit the streets like they used to do back when they did the street lottery and had to visit their customers. It took about two hours but they finally got some info on Leo.

"Let's go man, I know where he's at," Moe told Demetrius as they hopped back in the car.

Finally, Demetrius thought. It was eight at night, and he needed to meet this dude with the money by noon tomorrow. But Demetrius wasn't trying to wait until tomorrow to find his kids, he wanted them home tonight.

But when Moe pulled up at a nursing home and jumped out of the car, Demetrius wondered if he'd been on a wild goose chase. "What are we doing here?"

"Come with me, let's go see if the information I received is correct."

Demetrius got out of the car and stepped inside the nursing home. He immediately scrunched his nose. "Just tell me what's going on, I don't like the smell of this place and I don't want to be in here with all these old people."

"You do know that you're going to be old one day too, right?" Moe laughed at him.

They entered room 208 and stood in front of the bed of a very old, frail and sick man. Moe said, "Hi Mr. Leo, we came to check on you. How are you doing today?"

Leo hacked and coughed as he pulled the covers up to his chin. "I'm so cold. My mommy keeps it so cold in here."

16

Saul lifted his sword as a legion of angels joined him in the air. The enemy was waging war against the Shepherd family, but because of the constant prayers that bombarded heaven, God had sent him some serious help to defeat the enemy.

"Do they know who their enemy is yet?" the captain of the legion asked.

"Not yet," Saul informed them. "They are about to enter the field of death. Imps are standing guard and will devour them before they reach the boys if we don't take care of them."

The captain lifted his sword and clanged it against Saul's. "We will fight for all that is holy and all that is right."

~~~

"Why'd you bring us out here?" Demetrius asked his father as he and Moe pulled up to an overgrown field of nothing but weeds as far as the eye could see.

"There's a house somewhere behind all of these weeds. We need to find it and get inside. My gut tells me that the boys are here," Don answered his son.

That was all Demetrius needed to hear, he shot out of the car and headed across the street toward the field.

Moe got out of the car, but hesitated a moment as he considered the darkness of the night and the massive field in front of them.

"Don't y'all think we should wait until the rest of the crew shows up?"

Al lifted the gun in his hand. "We are the crew, now come on. Let's go get my nephews."

"Does anybody have a flashlight," Demetrius asked.

Al popped his trunk and pulled out a long flashlight that was so banged up, looked like it had been used to beat people over the head. It was like a multi-purpose tool.

They headed into the field, which looked more like a forest with all the weeds and trees. As they found a path to walk, Demetrius asked his father, "What makes you so sure that Dontae and Dam are here?"

"This field belongs to Leo. He used to bring cats out here to kill 'em. Lisa told me that many bodies have been buried out here," Don said.

Demetrius' head began to spin. This couldn't be another lead that takes them nowhere could it? "Dad, Leo didn't bring the boys out here."

"Look at this place." Don waved a hand at all that was before them.

"I would use a place like this, that's for sure," Al told them.

Demetrius turned to his father. "I'm telling you that Leo had nothing to do with the things that have happened to us. He's in a nursing home and he has Alzheimer."

"Then why would Lisa tell me about this place? And why did she tell me he was living with some woman."

Demetrius shook his head. "I Don't know…but I can guarantee you that the only woman Leo is thinking about is his mommy."

A loud noise cut through the darkness. Moe jumped, "What was that?"

"Sounds like a tree falling." Al told them. "Let's keep going so we can get as far away from that as possible."

If it wasn't for the fact that they were in these woods looking for his sons, Demetrius would have burst out laughing because he knew exactly why Al wanted to get away from any area where a tree might be falling. Many years ago, Don, Al, Stan and Joe-Joe got trapped by some thugs in the woods. They fought their way out, but they soon discovered that they wouldn't be able to fight against the wind and the trees in those woods.

A tree had come down on Don and Stan, crushing them so badly that they had to be hospitalized. Demetrius remembered how terrified Al had been at the thought of losing his closes friends. Demetrius also remembered that Angel's parents had been praying against Don and his crew that day, so God had not been on their side.

Angel was the one praying today, so Demetrius could only hope that the trees would fall on the men who kidnapped his sons and not on any of them.

"What's up with all of this fog, it was a clear day, not a cloud in the sky," Al said as they kept walking, trying to find the house that was supposed to be on this overgrown field.

～～～

"Oh Lord, we thank You that You hear us, because we know that You always hear us when we pray. We thank You for bringing Dontae and Dam home safely. And Lord we thank You for allowing Demetrius to see God at work in the rescue of our sons," Angel prayed.

"And Lord, we thank You, because we know that you have already made a way for the truth to come out about what happened to Dodi. Angel and Demetrius love their daughter and all of their sons, unite them again, Father, in Jesus name I pray," KeKe prayed.

Angel and KeKe prayed until they couldn't think of nothing else to ask God for. At that point, they began thanking Him for being the wonderful savior, counselor, redeemer that He was, is and always would be. They prayed so long and so hard that at one point Dee started crying.

As the tears ran down Dee's face, he opened his mouth and gave the Lord praise. "Lord, You are so good to me, I have so much and I don't even appreciate it. Help me to make better choices for my life, Lord. Help me to make my parents proud."

Little did Dee know, Angel couldn't have been more proud, than she was at that very moment. "God is good!" she shouted as she raised her hands in total praise.

~~~

The first blow came from Saul as he swooped down on the imp guarding the house where Dam was being held. The imp was spewing out a fog that covered the house and trees around the house.

"You will not defeat us, for we are many," the imp proclaimed.

"You were defeated the moment I arrived," Saul told him as he lifted his sword and gutted the imp.

After that the fight was on. Angels descended from on high slicing and dicing. The imps fought back, they weren't about to just give in and slink away, not when the destiny of the Shepherd family was at stake.

It seemed to Saul that as they dispensed one imp two more appeared. He wasn't about to fight these demons all night because he needed to clear the way for Demetrius to get to his sons. Saul stood on air as he lifted himself above the house. He also lifted his sword up high and swirled it around in the air until a vortex of wind was created. The demons and angels were pulled into the whirlwind and the angels took care of business.

~~~

Demetrius lifted his arm and pointed, "The house!" They had walked around this field several times, but with so much fog, they could barely see a hand in front of their face. But as the fog lifted the house came into view.

Just as soon as the house came into view, so did a big gust of wind that blew them this way and that way. Trees shook like they were about to fall. "What's going on?" Al yelled.

"Looks like some kind of wind storm," Demetrius responded as he stared in awe as a tree uprooted and flew off in the opposite direction.

"I don't know what's going on here, but I've been in a storm like this before and it didn't end well." Another tree fell, this one looked like it was headed in their direction. "Run!" Don shouted as he kicked up dust and ran all the way to the house at the back of the field.

~~~

Once those imps had been dealt with, Saul and his cohorts went down to the house and easily dispatched the evil minions standing guard at the door. "You will not stand in the way of Almighty God's command. The boy must go free," Saul told the burly, green eyed demon who stood in front of the door, blocking the entry.

"You gon' have to take me down like you took the others down. But I ain't no easy win," the demon told Saul as he prepared for the fight to come.

"So be it." Saul pulled out his sword and went to work. The battle intensified as the other angels attacked the last remaining imps as they hid throughout the house, waiting to wreak havoc on the Shepherd family.

Saul was able to get the humongous demon off the porch as he and the captain had planned. As Saul's battle with the demon intensified and they were rolling around in the field like wrecking balls, knocking down weeds and shaking trees, the captain of the host unlocked the front door and stood guard, to ensure no other demon would stop Demetrius quest to find his sons.

17

"What was that?" Moe asked as he fell to the ground.

"Felt like a strong gust of wind," Demetrius told his friend as he helped him up.

Moe shook his head. "The wind stopped a few minutes ago. Something just pushed me down."

They were standing in front of the badly neglected house. Which had once been painted white, but most of the paint had chipped off to the point where they were looking at grayish colored wood that had serious termite damage. So serious that the house looked as if it would soon collapse in on itself.

"Let's go in and check it out," Don said to them.

But Al said, "I don't understand why we're still here with all this weird stuff that's going on. Demetrius already told you that Leo don't even know his own name no more, so I doubt he's still plotting on getting even with you."

"I've got a feeling about this, Al. Lisa didn't tell me about this place for nothing. She knew something, I could see it in her eyes."

"You sure that wasn't just hatred for you that you saw in her eyes," Demetrius asked his father. "I was there. I remember how bad you treated that woman."

"Y'all can stand here chit chatting all night, I'm going in that house." Don walked up to the house and tried the door. It was unlocked so he stepped in.

Demetrius told Al and Moe, "Y'all hold it down out here while I go in with Dad to check things out."

"Grab that flashlight from Al," Don told his son. "I can't see a thing in this house and I know ain't nobody paid the electric bill in years."

With flashlight in hand, Demetrius lead the way as he and his father searched the house for Dontae and Dam. Demetrius had felt differently when these two boys came into his life. With Dontae he was a proud papa, passing out cigars and showing off his picture to any and every one he came in contact with. But when Dam was born, there had been so many unanswered questions that Demetrius didn't want anything to do with Dam. He'd even demanded that Angel abort the child. When she disobeyed him on that, Demetrius then demanded that she give Dam up for adoption.

Things may have started out bad with his youngest son, but Demetrius would give his life for Dam now. "Dam…Dontae… Dam…Dontae!" Demetrius shouted his sons' names as they moved through the house, hoping and praying that they would shout back to him.

They reached the kitchen and still, no answer came back to him. Demetrius' shoulders slumped in defeat. "I don't see any more rooms, Dad. Maybe Lisa didn't know what she was talking about."

Don heard a sound like something being banged together, he glanced out the kitchen window. A smile crept across his face. "Don't give up hope just yet, son. Come with me, there's a cellar out back." They walk into the backyard. And Don pulled open the cellar door.

Demetrius shined his flashlight and again shouted, "Dam! Dontae!" as he and Don made their way down the narrow stares.

~~~

"So when do you think those angels are going to show up? I'm getting hungry and I would love to sleep in my own bed."

"I know you're getting sleepy, Dontae, but you don't have to be sarcastic. God is real and angels are real too. Don't make fun," Dam admonished his brother.

"I'm not like you and mom. I don't always believe that everything is going to turn out alright in the end…I'm scared."

"It's okay, Dontae. I was scared too. But then I saw the angels coming for us and I knew that we were going home."

"When are they coming?" Dontae asked, eyes filling with hope.

Dam started to answer his brother, but then he heard something. Dam sat up, "Listen, I think dad is here."

Dontae jumped up and started shouting. Dam got up and tried to walk towards the sounds. But it was too dark. He tripped over some pots and pans making a loud clanging sound. Dam then picked up the pots and clanged them together as Dontae kept shouting.

Dam's arm was getting tired, he put the pots down and then he heard the creaking of the door above them.

"Is it Dad or the angels," Dontae whispered his question to Dam.

"I don't know, just keep yelling." Dam went back to banging his pots together.

Dontae yelled, "We're down here!"

~~~

Demetrius had never known happiness like the happy feeling he experienced when he descended the stairs of that cellar and found his sons. He grabbed his boys and hugged them like he'd never hugged them before. "Daddy's here…Daddy's here. I've got you and I won't ever let you go again."

"I'm so glad you found us, Dad. Dam was down here talking about some angels were coming to rescue us." Dontae shoved his younger brother.

"The angels did come. They were here, Dontae. I know they were."

"What are you two babbling about over there?" Don said as he stepped closer to the boys.

Dam ran over to him and hugged his grandfather. Pop-Pop, you're here."

"Of course I'm here. Didn't you pray to God about my parole. And it seems that God got me out of the joint just in time to help find you boys."

"Well, let's get out of here before the people who brought y'all here come back." Demetrius held tight to Dontae's hand and headed up the stairs with him.

Dam came up the stairs with his Pop-Pop while asking, "Why did Todd bring us here? Is he mad at you for some reason, dad?"

"Todd?" Demetrius questioned. Then he remembered that Todd had left work and didn't return today. He also remembered who had suggested he hire Todd. As they stepped out into the night air, Demetrius turned to his father. "I know whose behind everything that's been happening to us. You were right, this is about you, but not for the reason you think."

"Of course it's about Don," Lisa said as she and Todd stepped into view. "I hate everything about my dear ex-husband. Death is too good for you, I want you to suffer just as much as you made me suffer."

"I gave you everything you wanted. Nothing made you happy. All you wanted to do was drink," Don told her, not caring that she and Todd were pointing guns at them.

"You took me from the only man who ever loved me. You kept his money and you humiliated and destroyed a man who was a hundred times better than you will ever be."

"You told me he was cheating on you too."

"I lied…I learned how to do that from being with you all those years. She kept walking towards him, gun locked and loaded.

"Look, you want a shoot-out back here with me, fine. But let my grandkids go and you, me and Todd can go at it." Don had lived his life, he wasn't afraid of a bullet. But he was afraid for his grandchildren. For them he'd do anything. So, when Lisa told him to drop his gun, he and Demetrius did exactly as requested.

"Now get back into the cellar."

"No!" Demetrius shouted. "Let my kids go. They didn't do anything to you. Don't do this Lisa."

Dam nudged his father and pointed in the sky. "Do you see them?"

"Who?" Demetrius whispered.

"The angels, Dad. They're still here. We're going to be okay," Dam told him.

Demetrius then saw Al and Moe slowly round the corner. Al put a finger to his lips as he and Moe pointed their guns at Lisa and Todd. Demetrius breathed a sigh of relief figuring that the hand of man would surely save them. "Okay Lisa, we'll do as you say." He didn't mean it, but this was his way of explaining his next move, as he took Dam and Dontae's hand and scooted them over so they wouldn't be in the direct line of fire. He waited, thinking that Al and

Moe were about to shoot their enemies, but instead a strong gust of wind came.

The wind knocked the guns out of Al and Moe's hand and then blew Lisa and Todd closer and closer to the cellar door. Lisa and Todd moved as if they were being pushed each step of the way.

"No!" Lisa screamed as she and Todd fell into the cellar."

Demetrius ran over to the cellar and closed the doors. He then locked it and looked back at his son."

As the winds calmed, Dam smiled but said nothing. Demetrius shook his head. "Come on boys, let's go home."

No one said a word about what had just occurred. They glanced over at Dam every few steps, but they didn't question anything. The walk back to the car was long and Demetrius was just happy to be taking the journey with his sons.

Don came up on him. Put his arm around Demetrius and said, "Father and son back together again." There was a big satisfied grin on Don's face as he tried to hand Demetrius back the gun he'd laid down.

Demetrius refused to take the gun as he shook his head. "Not this time, Dad. I'm out."

"What do you mean, you're out. This is a family business, remember. I raised you in this life, this is all you know."

Demetrius didn't respond to his father. He kept walking, eager for the new journey with his wife and children. He was no longer trusting in the wisdom of his father. Somehow Demetrius knew that God would make away for his family…maybe he'd even start a business with his sons…Family Business 2.0.

Epilogue

Demetrius and Angel got up early on Sunday morning and went to church. He and Angel had much to thank God for. Not only were Dontae and Dam home, but the lab results had come back on Dodi's candy. The results showed traces of Fentanyl and after Detective Green was forced into retirement, the new detective on Dodi's case was able to locate the woman responsible for the incident. Most importantly, their baby-girl was back home where she belonged.

Home had took on a another meaning for Demetrius and Angel. Now that Don had taken over as head of the family business again, Demetrius decided that it was time for a new beginning. They packed up the house and were praying about which town would become their home. Angel was convinced that God had a purpose for their lives and Demetrius wasn't going to get in Angel's or God's way on this.

At church, Pastor Marks read from 1 Corinthians chapter 13:

Though I speak with the tongues of men and of angels, but have not love, I have become a sounding brass or a clanging cymbal. And though I have the gift of prophecy, and understand all mysteries and all knowledge, and though I have all faith, so that I could remove mountains, but have not love, I am nothing. And though I bestow all my goods to feed the poor, and though I give my body to be burned, but have not love, it profits me nothing.

Love suffers long and is kind; love does not envy; love does not parade itself, is not puffed up; does not behave rudely, does not seek its own, is not provoked, thinks no evil; does not rejoice in iniquity, but rejoices in the truth; bears all things, believes all things, hopes all things, endures all things.

The pastor continued reading in the book about love. Demetrius leaned over and kissed his wife on the cheek. All the years of their marriage, even when he was acting like a complete idiot, Angel's love never failed. She prayed for him, laughed with him, cried for him and waited for him. He couldn't let her or God wait any longer, so when Pastor Marks gave the altar call and asked if anyone was ready to give his or her life to Jesus, Demetrius didn't ponder upon what a wretched man he was because he finally realized that the love of God could erase all of that and make him a better man. He leaped out of his seat and made his way down to the altar.

As he walked, Demetrius replayed the eleventh verse of 1 Corinthians that Pastor Marks had just read. But this time he put himself in those scripture: When I was a child, I spoke as a child, I understood as a child, I thought as a child, but when I became a man, I put away childish things... I stopped doing those things that pleased my earthly father, and desired only to please my heavenly Father.

Tears streamed down Angel's face as she watched her husband lift his hands and give praise to God. Angel's hands went to her mouth as she lifted her eyes to heaven, in awe of what God had done for her and her family today. "To God be the glory," she muttered through her tears, "for the great things You have done."

The end of Book IV

Stay tuned for Book V, Servant of God coming in July 2017

Don't forget to join my mailing list:

http://vanessamiller.com/events/join-mailing-list/

Join me on Facebook: https://www.facebook.com/groups/77899021863/

Join me on Twitter: https://www.twitter.com/vanessamiller01

Family Business Series

Family Business I

Family Business II - Sword of Division

Family Business III - Love And Honor

About the Author

Vanessa Miller is a best-selling author, playwright, and motivational speaker. She started writing as a child, spending countless hours either reading or writing poetry, short stories, stage plays and novels. Vanessa's creative endeavors took on new meaning in1994 when she became a Christian. Since then, her writing has been centered on themes of redemption, often focusing on characters facing multi-dimensional struggles.

Vanessa's novels have received rave reviews, with several appearing on *Essence Magazine's* Bestseller's List. Miller's work has receiving numerous awards, including "Best Christian Fiction Mahogany Award" and the "Red Rose Award for Excellence in Christian Fiction." Miller graduated from Capital University with a degree in Organizational Communication. She is an ordained minister in her church, explaining, "God has called me to minister to readers and to help them rediscover their place with the Lord."

She has worked with numerous publishers: Urban Christian, Kimani Romance, Abingdon Press and Whitaker House. She is currently indy published through Praise Unlimited enterprises and working on the Family Business Series.

In 2016, Vanessa launched the Christian Book Lover's Retreat in an effort to bring readers and authors of Christian fiction together in an environment that's all about Faith, Fun & Fellowship. To learn more about Vanessa, please visit her website: www.vanessamiller.com. If you would like to know more about the Christian Book Lover's Retreat that is currently held in Charlotte, NC during the last week in October you can visit: http://www.christianbookloversretreat.com/index.html

Don't forget to join my mailing list:
http://vanessamiller.com/events/join-mailing-list/
Join me on Facebook: https://www.facebook.com/groups/
77899021863/
Join me on Twitter: https://www.twitter.com/vanessamiller01

Made in the USA
Lexington, KY
30 October 2017